The
Extraordinarily
Ordinary

BAKER STREET

Jean Goulbourne

LMH PUBLISHING LIMITED

Editor: K. Sean Harris
Cover Design: Roshane Anglin
Book Design, Layout & Typesetting: Roshane Anglin

Published by LMH Publishing Limited
Suite 10-11, Sagicor Industrial Park
7 Norman Road
Kingston C.S.O., Jamaica
Tel.: 876-938-0005; 876-938-0712
Fax: 876-759-8752
Email: lmhbookpublishing@cwjamaica.com
Website: www.lmhpublishing.com

Printed in the U.S.A.   ISBN: 978-976-8245-70-0

NATIONAL LIBRARY OF JAMAICA CATALOGUING-IN-PUBLICATION
DATA

Goulbourne, Jean
    Extraordinarily ordinary Baker Street / Jean Goulbourne.

    p. ; cm

ISBN 978-976-8245-70-0 (pbk)

1. Jamaican fiction.   2. Young adult fiction.
I. Title

813   dc 23

Prologue

Chains in the Dust

There you sit
With hand outstretched
Stupid, begging cringing wretch
Why do you beg, dependent fool?
Why have you become my footstool?
Your eyes are dull
Your mouth is shut
Your body slumps against the wall
I do not see your pain at all
I tell you no
The curses flow, I hate you
And then I see your crooked hands
Your feet bound by cruel bands
I see you shrink, I cannot think
Then a flicker dulled with time
Floats across your eyes
I now am wise
I feel your pain
I turn to you once again
Compassion swells
From a heart that was hard
I give and I regard
My brother in the dust
I must pull him up
I must!

Chapter 1

I am a sufferer, a big blighted sufferer and although the sun still shine, it nuh shine for me.

A Butter, yes, that was his name, sat under the coolie plum tree out in the yard at number 10 Baker Street in the inner city in Kingston, Jamaica, and wrote those words on a yellow writing pad. He was growing old, thirty-five years old his last birthday and this was a new year. Christmas had just passed and it had been a Christmas of limited funds and therefore limited food. No gifts as it always had been with him since his mother died many years ago, and he had avoided his own children as he had nothing to give them. It was hard to avoid them though when they lived at 26 Baker Street with their mother and he lived at 10 Baker Street. He remembered the littlest one looking up at him with longing eyes.

What could he do? He had not been able to pick any pockets lately and he begged but came up with just a few hundred dollars now and again. People were meaner than ever. Word had got around the area that he was not blind as he pretended to be and he was not lame as he also pretended to be. He was just a little too old to wipe windshields like he used to do. What could he do?

He wrote poetry and short stories but he could hardly get a thing published, just a poem now and then in the Sunday Views, and once he had got a prize in the yearly literary festival, but that was all. They had sent him cheques but he had had difficulty changing them as he had no bank account. Discouragement wreaked shadows on his face and the wrinkles around his mouth headed downwards.

A Butter stood and picked a few of the fruit from the tree that hung over the yard and popped them into his mouth. He knew it would give him a bellyache to eat coolie plums on an empty stomach but what could he do? He had to eat. He had gambled the last funds that he had in his pocket last night and he had lost. He would probably borrow again from his compadre down the road. He had to eat so maybe he could pretend to be sick or handicapped and go on the street to beg. After all, people from all over the city drove this way and only the people from the surrounding district knew about him. He was good at disguise. He felt he could be an actor but that was out of his league. He had begged now for years. Yes, that was what he would do. He would beg for a few dollars. *Man haffi eat a food*, he thought.

A Butter went into the tiny room and put on his begging clothes: a torn t-shirt, a pair of pants that was cut and jagged at the knee, and his oldest pair of shoes. No socks, that was unthinkable. He put his 'beggar look' on his face and fixed his hair which was already in locks. Now he was fit to go and beg a few dollars for his evening meal. He was hungry, but that was how it was. He was almost always hungry. He knew the landlord would soon be around for his own few dollars for the tiny room he rented from him, but who could pay the landlord? Hardly anybody living on Baker Street paid their landlord on a regular basis. In fact, many of the landlords around the whole area had lost their investments. Who could afford to pay them rent?

A Butter sauntered down the road and hit the main asphalted street. The road surface was hot and his pair of old canvas shoes with its rubber bottom caused the soles of his feet to burn. He knew how to get the people to give. He would limp as though his leg was crippled. He walked normally down the road and then he came to the stop light. The vehicles would stop there for the light to change and he knew how to beg with a limp just as he knew how to sit at the side of the road and pretend to be blind. A Butter started to limp as the stop light turned to red and he went out onto the road. The cars stopped. He saw a lady with dark glasses looking in his direction. He limped over between the cars and the lady turned up her window. No luck there even though she had seen his limp. He went over to another car and a man gave him a twenty-dollar coin.

"Thanks sah," said A Butter as humbly as he could but in his heart he mocked the man. *Limp you think me have nuh?* he thought to himself, *is A Butter dis, yuh fool yuh.*

By the time three hours had elapsed A Butter had collected three hundred dollars, enough to last him two days of rice and fried fish which he did not have to fry himself as he bought it already cooked from the cook shop nearby.

A Butter went to his room with the fish and rice after going to the cook shop and he had the meal. Then he took a bath under the stand pipe in the yard and donned some decent clothes. He had got these clothes this past Christmas from a second-hand sale at the local church and they looked quite respectable.

As he dressed himself he remembered little snippets of his childhood, like the old house he had lived in with his aging grandmother and an aunt after his mother died. He remembered the chickens in the yard and the ackee tree that they loved so much and the cedar tree that his mother had caused to be cut just before she died. The money from the cedar tree had gone to her funeral expenses. He had loved his grandmother but after she died his maiden aunt told him to leave the house and make his own living elsewhere. He was fifteen years old then and still in school.

A Butter had resolved to stay in school and learn. His teacher, Mrs. Morris, encouraged him in her classes and he learnt to write about his problems without a home to call his own. She gave him money to buy his food and gave him the clothes her own son had worn and left behind. She was kind and thoughtful, and he thought now of her kind eyes and her touch on his shoulder when he felt like giving up. When he left school at age sixteen she gave him a nice pen and a writing pad and told him to write to his heart's content.

He had written a lot but the trauma of living on the street in his young years had taken its toll on him. He remembered that he had not been able to get an exam certificate because he could not afford to pay the CXC examination fees so he had not taken the exams. He had no skills and no way of learning one. He had thought of carpentry or tailoring but no one would take him on as an apprentice. Life had been doubly hard for him without the skills he needed.

A Butter finished dressing and walked down the road. No limp now, just a triumphant saunter. He still had a few dollars in his pocket and he decided not to gamble but to hang on to it just in case.

He would join a domino game at the corner where he would play and hope that someone would offer him a beer at the end of the game. A Butter grinned to himself as he walked down the street and hailed some of his friends. Life could be good at times. Yes, life was good in spite of the hunger that he so often felt because he did not have a bang belly and he was as strong as an ox; so, yes life was alright since he could con a few dollars every now and again.

He wondered what Mrs. Morris would think if she saw him now, if she would recognize him with his straggly beard and locks. He had never been a real Rastafarian as he had never embraced the faith. He just had the locks as he felt it suited his lifestyle. A Butter had heard that Mrs. Morris was retired now and he wished that he could see her again and feel the soft touch of her hand on his shoulder.

"Hail the man," said his friend Gold Teeth as he joined them at the makeshift table on the seedy sidewalk. There was garbage on the street that the people who lived behind the zinc fences pushed out when they swept their yards. A few dogs walked up and down sniffing expectantly through the rubbish.

"Respect," answered A Butter as he sat on a stool the barmaid from a bar nearby provided.

The night was just beginning and he had money in his pocket. He hoped his companions would not hear the jingle of the coins as he played that night. He started to play with Gold Teeth, a master player as his companion. Winner and Blacka played against them.

As the domino game proceeded Gold Teeth and Blacka started to tease him as they did many nights when they played together.

"A Butter, how you get that name there?" asked Blacka whose skin was black and shiny under the street light, hence his nickname.

"At school you know," answered A Butter. "When one of the boys get in trouble them would pay mi to tell them a lie to use so that they could get out of it. The lie them did good and so them call mi A Butter because it was like butter 'gainst sun the way them get away and then mi surname a Butterfield. The name jus' stick."

"What kinda lie you used to tell?" asked Gold Teeth, grinning.

"All kind. Depend on the circumstances. But the lie them never fail yet. Them did good."

"You make plenty money off it?"

"Enough to feed mi and mi old lady and mi grandmother and aunt. They never always have it. Is so we eat sometimes."

"Then you nuh tell you mother how you get the cash?"

"Then you want her beat the daylight outa mi? Mi tell her mi wash the teacher car. She was a good woman you know. But she gone now. She in the sky somewhere."

The fourth member of the domino playing men was Winner. He had been quiet all this time. He was usually quiet except for when the horse he had backed was winning and he would scream with excitement, hence the name Winner as he knew the horses and he had come away a winner many times. He spoke now.

"So what is your formal name? The one you mother christen you with?"

"George Theophilous Butterfield," said A Butter as he pushed out his chest with pride, "only mi mother never really know mi father real name. It was a one-night stand and he was gone as soon as him done that night. Mi mother say she did like the name Butterfield so she put that on mi birth certificate."

"So you grow without a father," said Winner thoughtfully. "Like so many of we. Mi nuh know my father either. Soon as him hear say my mother pregnant him run way gone a foreign. Three women pregnant for him same time so them go work and throw partner. Is so mi grow up. Mi have three mothers and six brothers and sisters and no father."

"That good though. The woman them help them one another," said Gold Teeth.

"Is what you saying man? Is so half of Jamaica pickney

6

grow. Is the mother grow them, father non-existent or run gone like mongoose a run from dog," said Winner. "Then what 'bout you, A Butter? How many pickney Shawna have for you now?"

"She say mi have five sah. So she says. Mi a tell you mi try, but the pocket poor."

"So she still a make her demands?" asked Blacka.

"A what you saying man? Daily. The pickney want this, them want that as though mi make a money. You would believe mi is a billionaire the way she pressures mi," replied A Butter.

"Then you nuh think you should help her? You nuh remember you own fatherless childhood?" asked Winner.

"Mi remember yes. But what to do? Mi is a poor man. She did know that when she sleep with mi," said A Butter, adding in defence, "why she didn't use protection?"

"Why you never use protection?" asked Blacka.

"Mi nuh like them things deh. Mi nuh feel comfortable with them," answered A Butter, his voice rising a little in protest.

"So what about Shawna? She never have no father?" asked Gold Teeth.

"Shawna nuh have father or mother. When she was a baby her mother give her away to an old woman. The old lady help her till she dead when Shawna was sixteen and Shawna have to sell things on the street to survive. She good at business though cause the old woman who grow her was a higgler selling in the market and she teach Shawna to buy and sell. Shawna never go to school much but she can read and write and she good at the business side," replied A Butter.

Silence descended on the company as they finished the domino game and sat around drinking beer from the rum bar. Winner provided them with the beer as he sometimes did. There was a friendship between the four men as they were more or less all in the same position except that Gold Teeth had several baby mothers and many more children. They all judged their manhood on how many baby mothers they could control and how many children they had.

After the game A Butter walked up the dying street with his hands in his pockets. He was quiet as he thought about the conversation they had just had and the five children he had spawned. What could he do? Shawna, his baby mother, was sometimes so demanding that he was thinking of leaving her out of his life. Boy life hard. If he could get a job or a few poems published that would help him. He had tried but all had come to nothing. What to do? What to do?

A Butter walked up the street and paused under the electric street lights just for a while. He only had a candle at his home as the light had been cut off many months ago because of non-payment of bills. He shrugged his shoulders as though he was shrugging off the burdens that he felt had come upon him. *If only if only*, he thought, but he sighed as he looked at the street on which he lived with its zinc fences blotting out the view of the inside of the houses. His hand went up over his locks as he stood and viewed the scene in front of him. He thought that it must be around one o'clock in the morning. He would sleep late the next day and go down to see Shawna. She would demand money to send the children to school and he had none except the small change for his next meal.

He pushed open the zinc gate and entered the yard. He was the only one awake in the yard. There was no light in the other rooms. He found his key and opened the door to his small ramshackle room. There were sheets of paper everywhere that he had scribbled on and given up on in despair. A Butter took off his clothes and lay on the bed in his underwear.

The days stretched like years in front of him and the nights could be torment. He felt the music of words in his ears and he often reached for his pen and the yellow writing pad on which he scribbled his reflections. He did that tonight. He got up and lit the candle and wrote and then he lay back on the bed like a baby. To him writing was therapy, it eased him up a bit and helped him. But before he slept he thought about his five children and in particular that last baby who looked the most like him. If only he could do something for them. With a smile on his face but hurt in his soul, he fell asleep.

Chapter 2

When he awoke the next morning it was to the sound of someone pounding on his door. *Oh Lord not Shawna, not Shawna again*, he thought, as he turned the lock and slipped the tower bolt open.

When A Butter peeped outside the door, he saw his son Jason. He looked distraught. His clothes were worn and tattered. A Butter thought, *women these days don't mend clothes like my mother used to do. They throw away the old ones and demand money for new ones.* Then he looked at Jason, whose eyes were full of tears.

"What happen now?" asked A Butter.

"Mama sick bad," said Jason as he began to sob.

"What wrong with her?" asked A Butter, a feeling of alarm rising in him. *Shawna sick, she sick bad or Jason wouldn't be crying so.*

"Don't know," said Jason, still sobbing.

"A coming," said A Butter as he got dressed and closed the door behind him. "Come," he said as he put his hand around the boy's shoulders and walked with him down the road.

Everyone was now rising. Children were already on their way to school and women, mostly domestic helpers, were walking rapidly towards the bus stop to go to work. Older men sat on the sidewalk reading yesterday's newspapers and younger men were moving too. They were mostly construction workers or people who sold goods in stores downtown. The dogs were walking up and down the street sniffing at every food box that lay on the street and disappointingly walking away as they were all empty.

A Butter sighed as he walked, hoping against hope that everything would turn out alright, that Shawna would be ok and that his children could still depend on her. He felt lost as he looked down at his son who was busy wiping away his tears. He did not know how he would cope if anything happened to Shawna, and for the first time he realized that he did care about her and about the five small children even though he had to admit to himself that he scarcely knew them.

He thought of the possible reasons for Shawna's sickness and the cost of getting a taxi to take her to the hospital downtown. He hoped Shawna had money in the tin can under the bed. He had often borrowed from it when things got really hard. Shawna sold goods from a box downtown, often running when the municipal police spotted her. It was illegal to sell like that on the streets without permission.

The boy stopped sobbing after a while and as the two of them walked down the street, the cool air of January hit hard. When A Butter pushed open the zinc gate and entered he was really frightened at the number of people who were in the yard just standing helplessly. Silence fell as he entered and he knew that something was dreadfully wrong.

He walked up the brief steps and entered the door on his right. His children were wailing and Jason's eyes were wide as he started to cry again. Shawna lay on the bed. She was breathing but she seemed to be in another world. He had to get her to the hospital and fast, but how? He had no money to pay for a taxi and ambulances did not exist for people like himself.

He bent down and pulled the tin can from under the bed. It had some money. He put some of the money in his pocket and stepped outside glancing again at Shawna as he did so. *A coma*, he thought to himself as he looked at her lying on the bed. He knew he could not wake her. She had to see a doctor. Jason went out and hailed a taxi which came promptly and the people in the yard helped him put Shawna into the car. A Butter took a nightgown from her box of clothes and towels and a sheet, packed them in a scandal bag and he, along with one of the other tenants, headed to the hospital downtown. The children were crying and before he left, A Butter asked another tenant called Mammy to give the children something to eat.

The taxi man drove through the busy traffic and down to the hospital. Shawna was unresponsive but still breathing when the porter took out a stretcher and they carried her into the hospital's emergency department. About half an hour later she was examined by a doctor and he had her admitted. She was still sleeping deeply.

"Is she diabetic?" the doctor asked and A Butter was ashamed to admit that he knew so little about his children's mother.

He had no idea if Shawna had any medical problems. He only knew her to be the mother of his children and he knew little about his children except to assist with money when he could, which was rarely.

"We will see," said the doctor. "We will have to give her a blood test. We will have to run other tests too so hang around ok?"

A Butter stayed on the hospital grounds, hungry and frightened and terribly worried. Shawna had always been there for them. Now it seemed that she was maybe even dying. What was he to do? There were five children to support. He would have to do it alone. How could he? He could pick pockets and he could beg but could that provide sufficient support for five young children?

By the end of the day A Butter learnt that Shawna was diabetic and that she was in a coma but she would probably pull through. He went to see her during visiting time that evening and as she lay there on the hospital bed A Butter did something that he had not done for many years, he held her hand and prayed. A few tears fell and he felt like sobbing real hard but remembered where he was and that he was a man after all.

A Butter went back to Baker Street by bus and saw that his children were fed. The women were kind in that tenement yard and A Butter was also treated to a meal.

Before A Butter left the yard, Jason held on to his hand and asked, "Daddy, Mama going to die?"

"Jay, I don't know. Pray for her, all right?"

"Yes Daddy. Daddy we can go to school tomorrow and in the evening go look for Mama?"

Jason, the eldest, was only 14. The others were 11, 9, 7 and 5 years old, and were all of school age. He had to take care of them now that Shawna was in the hospital.

A Butter looked at Jason and reached down and hugged him. The child flinched at first at the unfamiliar gesture and then yielded to his father's touch of tenderness. As he left the yard that night A Butter hoped that he had forged a bond with Jason. The children were in bed as he hastened down the street to his own room. He hardly slept that night. When he did sleep he sank into a dreamless slumber and woke the next morning troubled and fearful. He faced the day.

He bathed, dressed himself and walked down the road to see if his children were ok. Mammy had taken care of them during the night and she was giving them breakfast when he arrived. He was relieved and also happy when she offered him some of the cornmeal porridge and a slice of hard dough bread. He had not had a hot breakfast for a long time. Now the problem remained, how to send the children to school that day? Mammy solved that. She didn't think the children should go as they were still traumatized. She said she would be in the yard that day as she wasn't going out, so she would take care of them. Mammy didn't work, her children who were overseas sent her money on a regular basis.

He relaxed a bit and left to take the bus to the hospital.

A Butter took the bus from the bus stop. It was full. People were going to work, children were going to school and as he travelled he thought about work and what it would mean because now he realized that he had to find something to do and fast. But what could he do? Where could he turn? He had no marketable skills. His dream of writing a book flew through the window like a lame pigeon. He wondered if he would ever get the chance to even read a book again. Reading had always been his passion and he often spent days in the Institute library downtown just reading.

The hospital grounds was full of people. The porters were everywhere. As A Butter walked in the smell of disinfectant hit him and he felt so nauseated he almost threw up his lovely breakfast. He would have to wait for visiting time, a security guard told him. The noise was everywhere and the smell was all over the place and A Butter's heart was pounding with fear. What if Shawna had died during the night? What then?

He had no phone, he would have called the hospital from home if he had one. To call from Mr. Chin's land line in the grocery shop meant money which he did not have. A Butter sighed. He could not even find the ten dollars to call from the grocery shop to the hospital. Where had the thirty-five years of his life gone?

A Butter left the precincts of the hospital and wandered up the road.

"What happen man?"

The voice was familiar. A Butter looked up. It was Gold Teeth. He looked concerned.

"You look like hurricane lick you," said Gold Teeth.

A Butter held down his head. "Shawna sick," he said. "She in the hospital. Mi nuh see her yet from morning. Mi have to wait till visiting time."

"Oh Lawd. Weh you a go do?"

"Mi nuh know," muttered A Butter, almost to himself.

"Come, take this," said Gold Teeth, offering him a hundred-dollar bill.

"Thank you, thank you," said A Butter as he put the money in his pocket. "One day mi will return the generosity."

"You and you big word them," said Gold Teeth, grinning. "Take care, you hear?"

"Yes man and thanks," replied A Butter gratefully.

He then made his way back to the hospital. It was visiting time and the security guard let him inside the building. With his heart beating hard he entered the ward and saw her. She was still asleep. He went and stood over her. She was breathing deeply and she looked beautiful to him lying there on the sheet he had taken to the hospital. Her head was on a low pillow and he felt a rush of love for her. He prayed to God that she would live and he made a promise to God to take care of her and the children if she survived.

A nurse came to him as he stood there. "How she doing?" he asked the nurse.

"Much better," the nurse replied. "You never know she had sugar?"

"No," he confessed. "I don't think she know either. She is mi baby mother you know. And to tell the truth that's all I know her to be, the mother of my children. I hardly know the children either. I feel bad 'bout the whole thing. Is only that I don't have no money or job or anything like that."

The nurse touched his shoulders. "Nuh worry. She soon alright and you can make it up to her. Here is your chance. Meanwhile take care of the children. They are yours and hers. You can't dispute that. So try."

A Butter nodded.

"She will be alright?" he asked again hopefully.

"Yes man. The doctors know what they doing. She will soon be alright but she have to take her medicines and watch her diet. It is important."

A Butter felt much better. Then he bent and kissed Shawna on the cheek. She was sweating in the heat but he didn't mind the sweat. He loved her.

When A Butter hit the road again he decided to go to the large market to buy food with the money that Gold Teeth had given him. He had to give his children food and that market was known to be cheap and the food good. He hoped that Mammy would cook it. It was getting cooler now in the evening. He walked the distance to the market going through the bustling downtown street amongst the higglers who peddled their wares on the sidewalk and the handcart men and boys who pushed their handcarts through the crowds up and down, up and down. He stopped for a while and thought to himself, *if I could get a hand cart, maybe I could make a living from it.*

"Move, move!" shouted one boy as he almost hit A Butter in the rump. A Butter scuttled out of the way. He saw what he wanted, callaloo and green bananas. He had not had that for months. He hoped his children would like it too. He used eighty dollars for the food and made his way to the bus stop. There was a tiny smile on his face. It was the first time in many months that he was really providing for anyone but himself and it felt good. He wanted to be a real father to his children. He was determined to start now.

A Butter made his way back to Baker Street and gave the food to Mammy. She cut the callaloo and peeled the bananas.

"How she doing?" Mammy asked as the children came around him.

"The nurse say she will be alright. Is sugar and she still in a coma but the doctors them know what they doing. So she will be alright but she have to watch her diet when she come out,"answered A Butter.

"Daddy, we can go see her?" Rhona, his eleven-year old daughter asked him.

"They not letting children like you go into the hospital like that," said Mammy. "They 'fraid you will catch disease."

Rhona wiped a tear and went into the room away from the family grouping around the coal pot in the yard.

"The children really feeling it," Mammy said to A Butter.

"I know. Mi feeling it bad too. Mi never even know that mi baby mother sick." A Butter hung his head as he said this.

"Is so life go," Mammy looked up and said quietly. "Now you have to take you responsibility seriously. Shawna had it hard you know. She used to talk to me. But Shawna love you which is why she stick by you. Nuff man would want her but is you she love."

The children had moved away by this, so this talk did not include them. Jason sat in a corner fiddling with a stick in his hands. The others went to join Rhona in the room. Mammy called them when the food was ready and they all ate. A Butter went home feeling like a dog with its tail between its legs.

Chapter 3

A Butter woke the next morning and looked at the sky from the window in his room. It was still dark outside but he felt propelled to move and go look for a job somewhere. But where? He did not know. He had no marketable skills that he could use to help him. He dressed and put on his shoes. There were holes in the shoes but they were all he had. He felt that he could go back to the market and help some vendors who might need him to move things.

The change in his condition felt burdensome this morning. He had a family to support now. He had had little thought of it before, Shawna had always been there for them. Now he had to find food and clothing and shelter for the five children he had spawned. He had to send them to school. What if Shawna died? It was a real possibility. A Butter sighed deeply. He felt overwhelmed but the children were his and Shawna was the woman that he loved.

When A Butter arrived at the market-place, most of the vendors were still sleeping. They were lying on the ground on mats and banana rush and crocus bags. But there was a man in the corner cooking porridge in a huge iron pot. He was preparing breakfast to sell to the vendors. The cook had dreadlocks and a graying beard. He stirred the pot with a huge aluminum spoon. He looked up as A Butter approached.

"Hail the man," said the Rastafarian.

"Respect," said A Butter.

"The man in some kind of trouble?" asked the Rastafarian. His voice was kind.

"Kind of," replied A Butter.

"Like what?"

"Mi baby mother in hospital and mi have to find food for mi pickney them. Mi nuh have no money and no job. Mi just want to find something to do. You know of anything?"

The Rastafarian was silent for a while. He took a plastic cup from a bag and put some cornmeal porridge in it. He handed it to A Butter.

"Here, drink this," he said. Then he looked at A Butter and asked, "You did go to school?"

"Yes, but mi never have the money to pay the exam fee so mi nuh have no certificate."

"But you can read and write though?"

"Oh lawd man yes. Mi all win award for poetry in festival."

"The man is a writer," confirmed the Rastafarian.

"Sort of," answered A Butter.

"Then you can do a test then?"

"Yes man," said A Butter, hope building in his chest as though it was about to burst.

"They looking for security guards in the security firm near here. They having the test down the headquarters. Maybe you can fit the bill, so try nuh?"

"When? What time?"

"Today at ten o' clock. Go try man. Here take this." He handed A Butter a hundred-dollar bill. "Feed you children till you get the job."

"Thanks, thanks. Lawd thank God!" said A Butter. He drank the rest of the porridge. He would buy some cornmeal and sugar with the hundred dollars and take it to Mammy, then he would put on his best clothes and head for the headquarters of the security firm. He knew where it was. He had to hurry. After the test he would go to see Shawna. He hoped that she was ok by now. Things were working out, well at least he hoped so.

A Butter went home after buying the food and giving it to Mammy. He took a bath and put on his best clothes. He cleaned his shoes with the flowers of the hibiscus plant and headed down the road. He had to walk. He had no more money to pay the bus fare.

The sun was getting up in the sky when he arrived at the place where the test was to be done. There seemed to be hundreds of men and women there all waiting to be tested for the job. A Butter's heart sank to the pit of his stomach.

The sun was hot overhead when at last they were called in to take the test. Some people grumbled as they were handed the papers and they were told to be quiet.

"Them must be think we a pickney," said one woman as she hissed her teeth. She got silent as she was asked to leave if she couldn't be quiet.

The group of people settled down at last. A Butter had to rack his brain to remember what he had been taught in school, but he had been reading at the library on a regular basis and his love of writing assisted him. He had difficulty with the math as he had never been very good at it but he completed the test on time and handed in his papers. They were told that the results would be out in a month's time and then there had to be an investigation to find out the background of those who had been selected. A Butter had no police record. In spite of the careless life he had lived, he had always steered clear of the police. He had never handled a gun or joined a gang.

As A Butter walked back to the hospital, a feeling of shame enveloped him. He felt that he was a failure. He had spawned five children who scarcely knew him and the woman who had delivered them to the world for him was sick in the hospital and he had nothing to help her. She had fed his children. She had clothed and housed them. She had given them the love that they needed and he had taken from her and given her no assistance in return. As he entered the hospital gate a feeling of fear gripped him. What if she were dead? What would he do? It was visiting time so he walked up the stairs to the ward and looked anxiously around the beds. There she was! She was awake and looking at him. She lifted her hand as she saw him and he rushed towards her.

"A Butter," she said simply.

"Shawna," he replied. He took her hand and kissed it.

"What happen?" she asked with surprise in her voice.

"Nothing. Mi just glad to see you, see that you all right and everything."

"Doctor say mi have the sugar. Mi have to watch what a eat from now on and take mi medicine."

"I know. And Shawna, mi trying to get a job. Security guard at the security firm. Mi going to take good care of you and the children from now on. Mi not going to play the fool any longer."

Shawna was silent for a long while and A Butter held her hand anxiously, waiting on her response.

"How the pickney dem?" she asked.

"Them all right. Mammy feeding them for mi. Mi buy the food, give her and she cook it for them."

"Mammy always a help me. She is a good woman," said Shawna.

"Mi glad say you wake up Shawna. Mi was fretting. But you alright? The food good?"

"Yes you know, it good and some of the nurse them nice. The doctor them work too hard though and the orderlies. Them do more work than the nurse them. Clean up the patient them and thing. Mi can leave the hospital next week. So you can tell Mammy and the pickney them. Mi glad to see you A Butter and that you take care of everything," said Shawna, smiling.

When A Butter took leave of Shawna that afternoon, it was with a feeling of hope. She would soon be out of the hospital but that did not cause him to forget his determination to be a real father to his children. He would be a real baby father to Shawna too, he thought to himself and then he remembered that he had no money and the children needed to be fed that evening. He too needed to eat and Mammy must be waiting on him to buy the food to be cooked. He put on old clothes and headed to number 10 Baker Street. He would go to the market and carry loads. He could earn a pittance there. It was dirty, hard work, but it was better than begging on the street. He was strong and he could lift the heavy baskets that the market women struggled with. He hoped that they would be generous to a newcomer like himself.

The sun was still hot and A Butter wished that he could lie in his little bed and sleep, but that was unthinkable now and he was hungry. The only thing he had eaten was the cup of porridge from the Rastafarian. A Butter smiled. Now that was a good, kind man.

A Butter passed the vendors on the road peddling their wares. He wished that he could buy an orange from the orange vendor but he had no money. There were people selling ripe bananas and coolie plums. A Butter walked briskly. He had to get to the market and fast, as his stomach was grumbling and he remembered his children back there on Baker Street.

It was about three o' clock in the afternoon when he arrived at the market and he hurried inside. *Where to begin*, he wondered as he looked at the crowds and the stalls with the food piled high. There were yams and sweet potatoes, cabbages and cucumbers, tomatoes and callaloo, scallion and thyme, cocos and dasheens, green and ripe bananas, food everywhere and not a drop for him to eat. He remembered the *Rime of the Ancient Mariner* that he had read in school and took heart that at least he had remembered something from his school days. He also remembered Mrs. Morris and her encouragement. He saw a woman looking at him. She looked kind. She had a load of food stuff in front of her and he went over to her.

"Mi just looking some work Mama," he said, "you have anything you would want me to do?"

"But see here. You want work? Just carry this bag go give Miss Brown for me. Mi can't leave mi stall and she waiting on the things. See she over there near to the door. And nuh thief nothing out of it you hear me? When you come mi give you a bligh."

A Butter did what he was told and earned fifty dollars. It was the beginning for him. That day he carried things to and fro and for the first time in a long time he carried home five hundred dollars of well-earned money. The lady whose work he had done when he just entered the market gave him some leftover cabbages and some yam and potatoes that had not sold for the day. She was going back to the country that evening and did not want the load. A Butter grinned all the way to Baker Street. He walked as he did not want to spend the money on bus fare. He would go back tomorrow.

Mammy cooked that night and A Butter ate with his children, seated on an old tree stump in the yard in which they lived. It was one of the sweetest dinners he had ever had. He went home that night, bathed and slept like a log.

It seemed like a new beginning and the end of a bad phase of his life. A Butter was happy.

For the next month he worked in the market carrying loads. The people he worked for often gave him the goods that were not sold and he took the food home at nights. Mammy cooked the food and he ate with his children. It was hard work and his back ached at first but he got used to it after a while. He visited Shawna every day in the hospital and learnt more about diabetes and how to live with it.

On Sundays he sought out his friends and played dominoes and drank beer with them. In spite of everything it was like old times. Winner was particularly supportive but Blacka and Gold Teeth showed that they cared and understood his dilemma as well. They often helped him out by buying beer for him when he simply did not have the money. It was a difficult time for A Butter but all his life had been difficult. He was no stranger to times of hardship and he realized that things had to improve. The only way was up, he could go no farther down.

At nights he was so tired that he fell asleep quickly but not without a few minutes of deep thought. What to do? What to do? Where to go from this? But deep in his heart he felt that things would improve.

Chapter 4

Shawna was coming home one morning in early February and A Butter went to get her in a taxi. The children were jubilant when she arrived home. They held onto her clothes and they hugged and kissed her. A Butter felt jealous. The children never hugged and kissed him. Shawna rested for a week and then was back on the street selling goods from a box. She took her medicine and watched her diet.

A Butter still went to the market and carried loads. He earned between five hundred and a thousand dollars a day. He was up early in the mornings and he went home in the nights. It was hard going but he was beginning to like working and the reward he got as a result. He was determined never to beg again or to depend on Shawna for help. He was going to be a man. He gave most of his earnings to the family to buy food and he ate from the family pot.

The children were back at school. Shawna saw to that. For the first time A Butter began to take some interest in what they did at school. He found out what grades they were in and if they got homework. He asked the names of their teachers and the name of the principal. He knew that Jason was going to the local upgraded high school and that the second child, Rhona, was about to do the Grade Six Achievement Test in March and that she wanted to go to a traditional high school. The other children, Julie and Roly, were in primary school and the youngest, Sean, was in a basic school run by the Pentecostal church that Shawna attended. A Butter was himself amazed at how little he knew of his family. He had regarded Shawna only as a sexual partner, hardly as the mother of his children. He had regarded his children as unimportant spawns of his indifferent lovemaking, hardly as his own offspring. Now he was beginning to know and love them.

One Monday, one month after the test at the security firm, A Butter got a letter in the mail. He had passed the test and was asked to come in for an interview. A Butter found Shawna and told her the news. She smiled at him.

"So you going to be a security guard now!" she said.

"Look so," he replied shyly. "Mi nuh know what to wear. Mi clothes them look so shabby."

"Mi will wash and iron them for you. Hold up you head man! Walk tall! A Butter you know that you change since mi get sick? You more caring," observed Shawna. Her voice was quiet, contemplative.

"Mi never really know say mi have a family and that you mean so much to mi. But now Shawna, things looking up and mi not going to go back down there in the valley; mi climbing the mountain and mi climbing with you and the pickney them."

"Alright man. But you have to help me with Jason. Him getting difficult."

"Like how?"

"Like him rebelling. Want to join gang at school."

"Who tell you?"

"Him form teacher, Miss Samuels."

"We have to go deal with that one," said A Butter in deep thought. "Mi can't make mi son turn gunman on mi. Bad as things be mi never handle a gun yet."

"Mi know A Butter. Why you think mi stick wid you? You never one day lift a hand to beat me or anything and that is what happen to so many woman down here. Them get bad treatment from them baby father."

"But mi never really help you with the pickney them. Is just now mi trying. Mi telling you Shawna, sometimes mi feel bad how mi never give you a thing and you a struggle so with them." A Butter felt real shame.

"Nuh worry. Now you a change and I just hope you will keep it up. Now, about Jason, you a go talk to him?"

"Then nuh mus'. Mi have to talk to him yes. Nuh mi son?"

Shawna smiled. This was the first time she had heard those words from the father of her children. She sensed a real change in him and she wondered if he really loved her. She loved him in spite of everything because she saw a good streak in him. It was as though he had not realized the goodness that was in him. It had taken her sickness and hospitalization to bring out a little of it and she was happy about that.

Shawna collected his clothes and washed them and ironed them carefully. A grateful A Butter took them and put them in his room in preparation for the interview which was the following week Monday at ten o' clock. He decided to spend some time with Jason over the weekend. He had to get the gang business out of that boy. Now that things were looking up he had to make sure that his children benefitted from it.

Meanwhile he went to the barber and got a trim and a proper shave. A shoemaker repaired the holes in his shoes and he cleaned them till they were shiny although not like new.

He called Jason just after breakfast on the Sunday morning. A Butter was sitting on the old tree stump in the yard at 26 Baker Street. Jason was timid as he approached his father then turned defiant when he guessed what his father was going to say to him.

"Jason," said A Butter, "I hear you misbehaving. Is true?"

"Misbehave? Them a tell lie pon mi. Mi nah trouble nobody. Mi only with mi friend them. We nah do nothing bad. We just a enjoy we self."

"Jason," A Butter's voice was low, "you know what friends can lead you to? Why you think mi never go to prison yet? Mi mother and mi grandmother teach mi 'bout friends how when them bad, them is trouble. You have to choose you friends. Now what you and the friends them doing?"

Jason's eyes blazed with anger.

"How come you care now? When you never care 'bout we before? What kinda father you think you is? You might as well be in prison the way you used to treat we and we mother. You never care anything 'bout we! How come you start to care now? You tell me."

Shawna came out of the room and faced the angry child.

"Jason. Nuh matter 'bout the past. It gone. Him is you father. Respect him," she said.

"Respect him Mama? How mi fi respect him? Him all go street go beg. Him a carry load a market and him nuh care 'bout we! Why you breed for him Mama? Why?" Jason was sobbing as he said this.

"So you shame a me Jason?" asked A Butter. "You shame of you father? Well now you join gang you going to kill me too? Eh Jason, you going to try to kill me?"

"Mi hate oonuh. Mi hate the whole of oonuh. Sometimes mi so hungry mi can't even sleep. What oonuh have mi fah? Mi want a different father. Not this one. Mi want a father who though him poor, him care 'bout we."

Shawna was shocked. She broke a whip from the tree in the yard and ran after the child.

"Enough Jason, enough. Him is you father you hear me? Him is you father so you mustn't shame of him. And now him is trying. Him is trying now, so help him!"

"Help? Help him Mama? Mi woulda rather help a dog. Help him? Him nuh help mi!"

Shawna grabbed the child and started to hit him with the whip. He screamed as the whip hit him all over.

"Nuh talk to me like that!" she said as the whip laced his body and Jason screamed in pain.

"All right Shawna, nuh bother. Lef' him. Lef' him now. Him shame a me." There was pain in A Butter's voice as he said this and he turned and walked through the gate.

The other people in the yard stood watching the scene. Mammy went to Shawna and took the whip. She held the whimpering Jason to her breast and said to Shawna, "You go lie down now. You just leave hospital. You have sugar. Mind you collapse."

A Butter walked to number 10 Baker street, entered his room and sat with his head in his hands.

Distress was etched in every line on his face. He had failed. He had failed his son and his baby mother. He had nowhere to turn except to his friends and where were they now? Gold Teeth was gone to look for work. He hadn't seen him or Winner or Blacka for some time. He wished that he had someone to talk to, someone who would understand. But there was nobody.

A Butter sat there for a long time. He didn't eat that day and he scarcely slept that night. At six o' clock the following morning he heard a knock on his door. He dragged himself out of bed and went to open it. It was Shawna. She was distressed.

"Jason run weh. Mi can't find him," she said and fell into his arms. A Butter held her close.

"We have to tell the police," he said, "mi have to find him, mi have to make it up to him, to all of you. Mi never know how much mi could care Shawna. Mi never have father either. Everything was mi mother and grandmother and them dead and gone. Come, come lie down. Mi will inform the police."

"Remember you interview this morning," said Shawna.

"I know. That is at ten o'clock. Mi will reach in time. Lord Jesus help us. Help us please."

At the police station, A Butter described the child, what he was wearing, and handed them a photograph that Shawna had pressed into his hands. The police promised to send out an alert in the next forty-eight hours and to put the picture on the television if Jason had not returned in that time.

Shawna was sleeping when he returned. He did not wake her but dressed and went to the interview. He was determined to get the job. And he did.

Even before the interview was over, he was informed to come in for his measurements for uniforms and for training. The interviewer mentioned the fact that he spoke English well in the interview and that his grade for the test was good. He had high hopes for him. Even though A Butter spoke Creole he could also speak proper English and he knew where to use both languages and when they were required of him.

A Butter left the compound with mixed feelings. He felt like a failure and yet there was hope. He returned to his little room and found Shawna there. She had tidied the room and put all his clothes which had been scattered, on clothes racks. There was some food in a plastic container. He was pleased.

"Where the children?" he asked her.

"Gone to school," she replied. Then he told her of the interview and his apparent success. She put her arms around him and held him close.

"A Butter I was always fretting that you would leave me. You going to stay with me?" asked Shawna.

"Shawna is nobody but you. You is mi first and only girlfriend. Mi can't leave you and the pickney them, not now, not ever. Mi see how you stick by mi when mi was nothing but a pickpocket and beggar. Now Shawna, mi all want to married to you. Is just so mi feel."

Shawna held him tight.

"Thank you Jesus," she said quietly and he kissed her.

Chapter 5

On the morning of his first working day, A Butter eased himself from his small bed, stood and stretched his arms above his head. He had had to drink soursop leaf tea to calm his nerves last night. Jason had still not been found and Shawna was still distressed when he left her with the other children. Shawna felt that it was her fault, because she had whipped him. A Butter felt that it was his fault as he had been a really neglectful father and they had had a bit of a fuss about it before he found his way home, got the soursop leaves, made the tea, and got into bed that night.

He had heard his clock ticking and the wind outside had sounded loud. So had the cars that passed his window with the light from the headlamps shining through and disturbing his sleep. It was still dark outside and the air was cool when he got up. He knew it would be hot later on but January had passed and February had just begun. Even though it was a tropical country, these were relatively cool months for the island.

A Butter heated water on the oil stove in the corner and

fixed some breakfast. He ate and bathed at the stand pipe out in the yard then he donned his new uniform and put on his shoes.

He felt like a new man with his newly mended shoes and his immaculate uniform. He combed his closely cropped hair and looked at his fingernails. They were clean. He looked at himself in the small mirror and felt that he looked ok. He vowed to throw out the clothes he had often used for begging and swore never to wear them again. He had a job. It made all the difference to a young man like himself.

Jason had eluded the police and even though they searched and asked questions, he was nowhere to be found. A Butter had bothered the police at the station till they were tired of him. He had made enquiries everywhere, even in the market where he had found work before. Nothing, nothing at all. Where could Jason be? Where?

The sun was peeping out from its nightly hiding place when A Butter stepped out from his little room, shut and locked the door, and walked down the street. He, George Theophilous Butterfield, was going to a respectable job. It was the first time in his thirty-five years that he had been so favoured and he remembered Mrs. Morris, his teacher, who had had such faith in him. He made up his mind to write something on the yellow writing pad that night when he came home.

He had to walk to work. He couldn't even take the bus. Not yet, not until he received his first payment at the end of two weeks. It was above the minimum wage and for him, A Butter, it was a massive amount. A cheque of over ten thousand dollars was a lot of money for someone who used to beg on the streets. He would start an account at a bank and also the credit union. He often heard that it was easy to borrow from the latter institution and one never knew when a loan would be required to help out a situation.

Children in uniform were making their way to school. Domestic helpers who worked in rich people's houses were already at the bus stops and the vendors selling oranges and ripe bananas. The beggars were also out. Cars were everywhere and the buses lumbered up and down the busy streets stopping at some bus stops and picking up people on the way to their destinations. A Butter was on the way to the headquarters of the security firm to be assigned to the place that they would first place him. He had received basic training for the job, but he was a bit nervous and he was determined to succeed, if even just to please his son Jason when he returned, because A Butter was sure he would return soon even if it meant that he, A Butter, had to find his hiding place and flush him out.

When A Butter arrived at his workplace he was of two minds. He was sweaty and full of trepidation. He had lost his freedom. He was now employed. He had children to care for. His baby mother needed to be cared for. He had other responsibilities rather than himself. He wanted to run and hide.

But another mind invaded his senses. You are now a man. You have a job. You have a family and a woman who loves you. You will walk tall now. You no longer beg on the street or depend on others to feed you.

And the latter voice prevailed. Once again he remembered Mrs. Morris and he smiled.

He walked up the stairs to the place where his boss would tell him what to do and he walked tall and happy. He was actually earning money legitimately and he could feed his children at last.

He was assigned to work in a bank to keep his eye on customers and those who might come in to rob them. He had no gun. He was just to keep watch. The hours were long because he had to work even after the bank closed at 2 pm. It was usually an eight-hour day but sometimes he would be asked to work a twelve-hour shift. He had the weekends off.

A Butter was transported to his place of work in a van and he entered the bank and joined the other security guards who were dressed like him. They greeted him and for the first time A Butter hoped that nobody would recognize him as the young man who begged on the street in old clothes. He felt ashamed of what he used to do now that he was a real man.

The doors of the bank were open at half past eight and A Butter watched the people come and go. His mind ran on Jason sometimes in the long day and he wondered what to do to get back his son. He wondered if he was dead or alive, what he was eating, where he was sleeping, and in spite of the feeling of happiness about the job, his runaway son weighed on his conscience, on his mind, and he wished he could do something, anything, to get him back.

He knew now just how much his children needed him and remembered how bereft he himself had often felt without a father's guidance. Was Jason begging as he used to beg? Was he washing windscreens as he, A Butter, used to do sometimes before? Was he learning to pick pockets? It left a bad taste in his mouth, the idea of his son behaving as he had behaved.

At lunchtime, A Butter had a callaloo loaf and a small bottle of drink. And after an uneventful day at the bank, he headed home. On the way home he remembered that Rhona was going to do the Grade Six Achievement Test in a month's time and he wondered if he remembered enough to help her. Yes, he was going to try. After all, he had done well in the tests for this job. He was not too rusty.

That evening, A Butter walked home even though he was tired. It was no joke just standing and keeping watch all day. But it was a job and at the end of two weeks, he would get paid and he knew that he had to stick by it for the sake of his children, his baby mother and himself. The days were still short so by six o' clock it was getting cool and the darkness was not far away. People were still on the streets. The vendors were trying to get the last dollar to carry food home to their children, young men were lingering before they turned in, some working as pickpockets, others smoking a spliff, others just watching the girls go by as he used to do.

How things have changed for me, A Butter thought. *Now I am a working man. I no longer have to beg or depend on others for food.* It had been just a few weeks and everything was different. He smiled to himself as he turned onto Baker Street.

I wonder if I will live somewhere else? Somewhere better, somewhere where I can invite some friends for a drink? he wondered as he walked down the grimy, dirty Baker Street.

A Butter saw Winner coming up the street towards his gate and he paused. Winner didn't know yet that he had got a job and was working. It was some time now since the last domino game and so much had happened since then. He knew Winner would be happy for him. He noted the frown on Winner's face as he came towards the gate and stopped.

Winner gave him a hearty slap on the back but still looked serious.

"Mi glad for you man but you see you son that run weh yet?" So Winner had heard about Jason. He had heard about the job too.

"No sah. Not a word. The police nuh seem to want to look for him and mi nuh know how him managing now. Him young. Him just fourteen. Winner, you hear anything? You see him? You see Jason?"

"Mi hear that him on the street up on Hope Road wiping windshields and begging. Mi hear that him dirty and need a bath but him nuh seem to care anymore. Him have plenty friend but them not good. Them leading him astray.

A Butter we have to find him. Mi nuh always go to them uptown place there but we have to find him before him get in trouble and land himself in a lock-up. Him is only fourteen as you say and the police trigger happy."

A Butter felt as though every cell in his body was falling to the ground. It was as though his heart fell to his feet and stayed there. He could not move. He took some time to talk and when he did anger laced every word that he spoke.

"If them touch mi son, mi going to kill them."

"No Butter, no. Nuh commit murder. You must never be guilty of that. We have to find Jason and look after him properly. Mi will help you look. You is mi friend and mi sorry fi bring you this piece a news on you first day at work. So how was it? Good?"

"Good. Mi watching people in a bank. Watch fi see that everything work and no robber nuh come in come thief. It hard to be on you feet all day but is a job. So how you?"

"Mi alright. Mi a learn fi groom the horse them down on the race track. Mi a follow you example. Mi a go work as a groom when mi finish the training. You know seh mi love the horse them already. As you seh, is a job. How Shawna?"

"She alright you know. Have to watch what she eat and all that but she fretting 'bout Jason. Is her first pickney and she feel it cause a she did beat him. Lawd help mi and help mi pickney dem. Mi glad seh you going to help mi find him. You know Winner, things a change fi we. How Blacka and Gold Teeth? Them all right?"

"Them alright so far. No job yet but them a go on. You know how it go. Little by little. Well anyway, let me know if you hear anything. And no murder you hear me? Prison nuh nice and death row nuh sweet."

Winner left him at the gate and A Butter walked into the yard and entered his room. He changed into other clothes and then made his way down to Shawna's place to eat. He ate there regularly now and the children seemed to welcome his presence. He said nothing to Shawna as he feared for her health. He would keep the news to himself for the time being.

After eating a meal of tinned mackerel and rice, commonly called flash out, A Butter called Rhona to his side.

"Come Rhona, carry you homework. How the studying?"

"Some things me nuh understand," said Rhona, "GSAT hard, Daddy."

"Mi know. Mi can see that. But you can do it. You hear me? Mi will help you all I can."

"Thanks Daddy."

And so it was that Rhona and her father sat over the books that evening into the night while Shawna looked on with a smile on her face. She still worried about Jason's disappearance, but she had always wanted to see her baby father sit with his children and help them and guide them, and she was seeing that now. She had little education herself and now, at last, A Butter was coming around. Shawna smiled in anticipation of the many years ahead of them. There would be no more children. Five was enough but this was a relationship that she hoped would last as she loved A Butter and she loved her children.

Chapter 6

A nd so each day after work, A Butter went to see his family. He ate with them and helped the children with their homework. For two more weeks he heard nothing of Jason and the police seemed to have given up the search as there were so many missing children. Shawna still grieved and A Butter was sad most of the time. He was ashamed and humiliated but he held a feeling of hope that his son would return of his own accord.

He grew to love working at the bank especially after he received his first pay cheque and could hand some of it over to Shawna and start a bank account. As long as he had a job, he could eat and things were so different from the days when he went hungry some nights and faced the next day without a cent. If only he could find Jason and just talk to him, bring him around to see that changes had begun, positive changes. But the boy eluded both him and the police, and Shawna mourned as though she believed him dead.

Meanwhile Rhona was progressing steadily. She was learning from him and A Butter 'buttered' up his own mind as he taught her what he had learnt in school and at the library when he used to go there to read. The other three children became more interested in books too, and became members of the local library. The youngest, Sean, loved to draw and A Butter decided to nurture that talent that he saw developing. Sean was excited when after another two weeks of work, A Butter took home a drawing book, pencils and crayons for him.

Shawna smiled at the gift and handed A Butter a list of the dates of the children's birthdays, something that their father had never bothered to remember.

"Shawna, mi never even know your birthday. Which month you born?" A Butter asked.

"June. June 3rd," said Shawna with a smile. "It look like God make mi sick for a purpose. Now you paying mi some mind."

"Lawd Shawna, mi sorry. Mi just never know what to do. Mi sorry, believe mi. Mi going to make it up to you and the pickney them."

"A hope so," said Shawna, still smiling.

That night Winner dropped by.

"A Butter, how you do? You hear anything bout Jason?"

"Not a thing," answered A Butter. "Mi a look for him and the police them seem to give up. Him a hide."

"Gold Teeth see him with a whole group a pickney. Him a live on the street. When Gold Teeth ask him what him doing him cuss a big bad word and run. Is a gang of boys and them begging and a give plenty trouble. We have to do something. We can't make it go on so."

"Where him see Jason?"

"Uptown near Trafalgar Road," said Winner.

"A wipe windshield and beg, just like mi used to do when mi young. Lawd help mi. Mi son coming just like mi and just as things start to go good for mi, him turn vagabond." There was distress in A Butter's voice. "Winner what mi a go do? It can't go on so."

"If we could a get him to a reform school. That maybe would help. But we have to talk to him first," replied Winner. "Mi going to see what mi can do. Mi get to go uptown sometimes. Mi will see if mi see him."

"Alright. Thanks, you hear."

"Yah man. We have to do something for the youth."

Winner went away that night and left A Butter feeling like a nobody. Jason's reports from school had always been fair until he joined the gang and got into bad company. A Butter had seen the reports some weeks ago when Shawna had shown them to him. Now he was walking the streets. What to do Lord? What to do? For the second time in years A Butter decided to pray.

Two days later was a Saturday and A Butter took the bus uptown. He saw the boys and grieved as he knew the conditions under the heat of the tropical sun. He knew the insults that they faced and the insults the boys gave in return. He knew that it was a way to get into trouble in the end. The police would come looking for them and the beating would start in the lock-ups. He himself had been beaten once by onlookers when he stole a wallet from a man's pocket. That life was tough. It was difficult and it was not the way for any young boy to live.

He walked the length of Trafalgar Road but he saw no one like Jason. Where was he? Puzzled and in distress, he asked one boy if he knew him.

"Jason? Mi know plenty Jason. Which one yuh want?" asked the boy.

"Him dark just like me and him have a scar on him left hand right here so. Near the wrist."

"Mi nuh know you hear sah. Mi wi look but who mi to tell him a look fi him?"

"Him father. Tell him mi sorry. Please. What you name? Mi need to know so when mi come back mi will ask for you."

41

"Them call mi Mikey G. Everybody know mi. Jus' ask fi mi. Mi will see if mi can find the Jason yuh talking 'bout. But him fool fool. Mi wish mi did have a father or mi wouldn't be on the street. Alright sah, mi wi look fi him fi yuh."

A Butter handed him a fifty-dollar bill and Mikey G said thanks with a face lit up in a smile. Not many people had been kind to him like this.

A Butter went home that day but first he went to see Mammy. Shawna was downtown selling trinkets from her box. She had not stopped working even though she was diabetic. A Butter respected her independence but wished that she could do something better. She had to hide from the police to sell her goods. He decided that he would try to get her a stall in the arcade downtown.

Mammy greeted him with smile. "Is you A Butter? How you do? You alright?"

"Not so alright Mammy. Jason on the street."

"Mi know but mi nuh tell Shawna cause she will fret. Poor Shawna have to watch her health," replied Mammy.

"But is how to get him off the street. Is that a worry me now," said A Butter.

"Well bwoy we just have to wait and see if him will come back home. Mi hear seh you helping you children with them schoolwork. Mi would a like you help mi granddaughter, Marie. She not doing too well in school."

"Yes man, what grade she in?"

"Grade four. You ever think of teaching? Rhona say you can teach. She say she understand you better than her grade six teacher."

"Rhona say that?"

"Yes. Think 'bout it. You still young and plenty night school 'bout the place now. Do you exams and pass them. Mi would be so proud to know you."

"Mammy thanks for the encouragement. But mi too old now. Mi thirty-five the last birthday."

"A Butter you is a youth in the prime of life. Think 'bout it."

"Mi teacher Mrs. Morris, always tell mi that education is key and mi did try hard but mi couldn't pay the exam fees so mi leave school without the certificate." A Butter sighed." But things changing. Mi will think 'bout it. Send you granddaughter. Mi will help her."

"Thanks," said Mammy and A Butter left and went home to wash his clothes.

Chapter 7

The days slipped into weeks and there was still no sign or news of Jason. Shawna's anxiety increased and she seemed to be almost losing her mind. Her clothes went for days without washing and she could scarcely take care of her own health let alone that of the other four children. A Butter was constantly on call just in case she slipped into a coma again and he made sure that she stuck to her diet and took her daily medication. It was a difficult time for everyone and without the help of Mammy in the yard, A Butter did not know how he would have managed.

Rhona did her Grade Six Achievement Test towards the end of March and did not seem to have found it difficult. A Butter went to a parent teacher's association meeting and was pleased to learn that she had improved steadily prior to her examination. The teacher wondered if she had got outside help but A Butter just said that she did her homework and worked extra hard. He was reluctant to acknowledge his own input but he was quite pleased afterwards and was determined to help the others in his spare time.

In spite of the troubles at home at Baker Street, A Butter continued to work hard at the workplace. His immediate boss commended him once or twice for punctuality and devotion to duty. This was new to A Butter who remembered his old ways and he was happy to be recognized.

Then one day Gold Teeth brought him news. He had seen Jason and Jason had run across the road and into a gully when he saw him. Jason was indeed on the street with a whole lot of other boys who were being accused of theft and molestation of people on the road. Jason had on ragged clothes and a pair of dirty sneakers. His hair was uncombed and done up Rastafarian style and he looked much older than his age. He had a ratchet knife in his belt and the haggard look of a child whose life was in turmoil. Gold Teeth said that he had wanted to talk to him but he had run down through a culvert into a gully. Gold Teeth had no idea where he slept at nights as the gully was built to carry water away from the city when it rained.

A Butter passed on the news to Mammy but begged her not to tell Shawna anything. He was determined to find Mikey G and get the information from him if he could. On his next day off, he took the bus and went back to see Mikey G. A Butter went into the vicinity of Trafalgar Road and scrutinized the faces of the windshield cleaners to see which one was Mikey G. He saw him at last.

"Yow!" he greeted Mikey G when he saw him on the road.

"Yow!" answered Mikey G. Then he remembered the request as A Butter showed him a picture of Jason.

"Yes sah mi know him. Him live down the gully under some plastic. But him too bad, him no just beg like mi, him a t'ief. Him is a bad man. The police after him. Mi fraid a him sah. You better nuh do nutting 'cause him have a bad temper and him will cut you."

"Who him down there with?" asked A Butter.

"Some bad bad man them sah. Mi nuh talk to them and mi can't ask as them will cut mi. All them want now is a gun and them knife sharp and them use it if you nuh give them what them want," answered Mikey G, looking around in fear.

A Butter's face went from anger to worry, to fear and anxiety. His son was fourteen-years old and approaching his fifteenth birthday. What if the police shot him dead? The police was known to be trigger happy with people like Jason and they would kill if confronted. What if Jason got a gun? Would he come back to Baker Street to take it out on his own family? A Butter was distressed. He remembered the words his mother used to tell him. "Careful you know. When yuh t'ink a peace and safety, sudden destruction."

A Butter did not know where to turn. He couldn't tell Shawna. He couldn't tell Mammy anything more in case she spread it abroad. He had to find a way. But where? Who existed to help children trapped on the streets of Kingston? He looked up and saw the YMCA building just across the road. Would they help? He decided to try.

A Butter made his way across the street through the traffic and went to the building's gate. There was someone manning the gate. A Butter looked inside at the swimming pool and the old building beside it, and he felt hopeful. His mother had mentioned the work of the YMCA many years ago. Would they help him now? He approached the gateman.

"Morning," he said.

"Morning," replied the sleepy, grouchy gateman.

"I just need some help with mi son. Him drop out of school and living on the street. I just need to know if the people here will help mi with him," said A Butter hesitantly.

The gateman woke up. He too had had the assistance of the YMCA. He was an old boy of the institution.

"Come," he said. "Come in. They will do what they can do, where the boy? And how old him is?"

"Him on the street up the road and him is fourteen. Him run weh."

"Go in and ask for Miss Allman. Tell her everything, is YMCA did help me. Mi was a street boy too."

"Thanks. Thanks you hear. Miss Allman nice? Is she in charge?"

"Miss Allman nice like gold. Yes man, is she in charge. She will help you out. Just go talk to her."

A Butter went in and approached an office door. It was open. He looked in. He was afraid.

"Come in," said a young lady who sat behind a desk.

A Butter went in.

"I would like to speak to Miss Allman," he said.

"Please sit down. Let me ask her." The young lady went into another room and then came out again. "She will be with you in a minute," she said.

A Butter sat on the only other chair in the room and then he was called into another room.

Miss Allman had gray hair and a round, kind face. She sat on a chair behind a desk full of papers. She smiled at him. A Butter was no longer afraid.

"What can I do for you?" she asked.

"I just need help with my son. He is on the street and he is only fourteen. He dropped out of school."

"How can we find him?"

A Butter took the photograph from his shirt pocket and gave it to her.

"I hear he has locks now. He lives in a gully up the road. Please help him. Mi want back mi son."

"Tell me everything," she said simply. A Butter poured his heart out and she listened intently.

"We will try," she said when he had finished. "Can I keep the photograph? We will need it. How can we get in touch with you?"

"Yes Miss, you can keep the photo," answered A Butter.

He told Miss Allman of his workplace and the telephone number there. He spoke like a child to his teacher. He knew that he respected this woman with the graying hair who sat there behind the desk.

Then he said to her, "Please don't tell him that is mi who ask you to help mi. I wasn't the father I should be and him hate mi now."

"Ok we will keep the whole thing from him. We will just tell him that someone cares. Alright?"

"Thanks, Miss Allman. A really glad to talk to you. A know you will help mi. Thanks."

A Butter went home after thanking the gateman. He walked down the bright, sunlit street on the sidewalk until he came to a bus stop. He took the bus home and thought of the vast difference between the uptown dwelling places and the inner city houses. There was a vast change of scenery in the same town as one travelled from one end of the city to another. He had read some parts of a book called Two Jamaicas on his visits to the Institute library in the past and it now occurred to him that the book was so true. The lives of the people on Baker Street and those in the uptown houses were markedly different. Yet they were all Jamaicans.

He saw Mammy on his return but said nothing to her. Shawna was downtown. He went and bought food at the nearby cook shop and took it to Mammy to give his family when Shawna returned that evening. He then ate a patty and went home to lie down on his bed.

It was while he was lying down that he remembered what Mammy had encouraged him to do. Do your exams. Get a skill. *Could he do that?* he wondered. He remembered Mrs. Morris and her wish for him to succeed and he thought of his children and the quarrel he had had with Jason. Jason had been ashamed of him. How could he remedy that? What could he do? Could he at this late stage become a teacher?

A Butter slept and when he woke it was late in the evening. He got up, bathed, ate some food and went back to sleep. Before he slept he felt some hope in his heart but there still lurked the feeling of fear. Would Jason turn away from the life he was living and come home? Would Miss Allman be able to help? He could only wait and see.

Chapter 8

While Shawna worried about Jason, A Butter kept the secret from her. He did not want her to know so he dedicated himself to the children that were left behind. Roly, his second son, wanted to be a mechanic and he was still in primary school. Julie was his second daughter and she wanted to be a chef in a hotel. Sean loved to draw and drew everything in his sight. He was so happy when his father, whom he had scarcely known before Shawna's illness, gave him the tools to help him.

Many evenings he went to help the four children with their homework and then others came: Mammy's grand-daughter Marie and other children in that tenement yard and other tenements on Baker Street. A Butter's fame grew. Soon he was no longer A Butter even to the other adults around him but Mr. Butterfield. Mr. Butterfield's head was held high as he walked on Baker Street. There was a new spring in his step and he studied the books that the children loaned him in his bed at nights and went to the parish library sometimes to help him to get the knowledge that he needed now. He read voraciously. It was difficult sometimes to keep up as he had to work. There were times when he was dead tired but he was feeling not like a sufferer, but like a new man with a future ahead of him and children with futures he had to take care of.

Throughout the month of April, he communicated with Miss Allman on the phone at work. Jason was frequently spotted but was not yet persuaded to change his way of life. He seemed resentful when asked to come, but hunger seemed to be stalking him. A Butter knew that there were times when Jason went hungry as he himself had often done during his time on the street.

Jason was also a newcomer and therefore was being tested by the older boys. He had to prove himself to them that he was capable of enduring as they had done. A Butter knew how dangerous that was. Some gang members were asked to kill in order to really become a legitimate member of the gang. A Butter hurt deeply inside when he thought of this and the possibility that Jason would be shot before he ever saw him alive again.

On a day off he went back to the YMCA and saw Miss Allman. She smiled as her secretary showed him into the room.

"I have good news for you," she told him.

"You persuaded him?" A Butter asked.

"Yes, last week. He seemed to be tired of the street and really hungry so he came in to ask for food and something to wear. He was really ragged. I gave him some food and clothes and he seems interested in leather work and other craft work, and he wants to learn how to swim," replied Miss Allman. "Of course we did not make any mention of your part in it but he is coming along. We hope he will continue. He seems to have a temper though. We have to watch that."

"Temper? What him do?"

"Likes to fight. Fought another boy because he called him 'beggar boy'. But he came around and they made up. The boy was teasing him, you see. We told the boy to lay off and things settled down a bit. What else happened at home? You didn't tell me," asked Miss Allman kindly.

"I was a beggar on the street and I wasn't taking care of the children or the baby mother so he cursed me and his mother beat him and told him to respect me. So he ran away. Then I got a job as a security guard." A Butter hung his head as he said this.

"Things are looking up for you now though. Chin up! It will work out. We all have our failures and our successes. In fact, everyone fails at some point, even the most successful persons fail sometimes."

A Butter smiled. "Well I hope so. A trying Miss Allman. A sorry that a never know my children till now. I never knew that I love mi baby mother till now. I love them. I want to take care of my family. I never had a father. My mother and then grandmother grew me and they never have it so I grew up poor. I go to school and I learn good but I fall down 'cause I never have no certificate to show for it. I don't have family outside of these children and the baby mother."

"Keep on trying. You young. You will make it." Miss Allman reached out and shook his hand.

A Butter stood. "Thanks Miss Allman. Thanks. You think you could give him something for me?"

"Something like what?"

"Like soap and toothpaste and a rag to bathe with? I want to do something for him but I don't want him to know."

"Good. I will do that," answered Miss Allman, taking the money that A Butter handed over to her.

"I want to give him something every time I come. Just to let him know somebody cares about him."

"Good. Now you are being a father even though you never had one yourself. Keep it up. I respect you for this." Miss Allman smiled as she spoke.

After that A Butter went to see Miss Allman regularly and gave her some money to help Jason. He never saw Jason on his visits. Miss Allman took the money and he knew that she gave Jason the things that he needed.

Miss Allman told him one day that Jason was puzzled. Why was she giving him these things? And who was giving her the money to give them to him? But she told him nothing about his father's visits and his role in getting him into the YMCA. Jason had his good points she told him, he just needed guidance and he needed to build his self-esteem.

A Butter hung his head when she said this, feeling that it was all his fault. The boy never had a positive male role model which was why he took to gangs on the streets. He still tried to do his best though it hurt to hear what was happening to his child.

April slipped into May. The year really seemed to be catapulting its way into summer. A Butter kept on going to work and helping his children at home. The regular hum drum of life continued on Baker Street. A Butter went to PTA meetings with Shawna whenever he could. His children were improving and the teachers wondered where they were getting the help.

"Dem father helping dem," Shawna told them proudly and A Butter would smile and look bashful but he was pleased at the comments.

Chapter 9

A Butter received a call on the telephone at work one morning in early May. It was Miss Allman.

"Mr. Butterfield?"

"Yes, Miss Allman," he replied.

"Mr. Butterfield, I am afraid it's not good news. Jason used his knife and cut another boy. The police have taken Jason into custody. They are suggesting that he go to reform school. He is too young to be locked up. What should we do? I remember you didn't want him to know you were involved."

"Is the wound serious?" asked A Butter; his knees were weak and trembling.

"Oh it's not life threatening or anything like that. The boy went to the hospital and was treated and sent home. But Jason is an angry child. He needs to learn to control his anger. He needs to calm down Mr. Butterfield. There are counselors at the reform school who could help him. What do you say?"

"Please send him. I wish I could talk to him but I am the reason he is so angry. Please see what you can do for me and thanks. Thanks for everything you do."

"Ok I have your permission now but I would need something in writing from you as early as possible, can you manage that?"

"Yes Miss Allman. Of course. I will let you have it in writing."

A Butter went through the motions with a heavy heart but reform school meant that Jason would learn a skill and improve his reading and writing skills. The boy had ability. Anyone could see that and he knew that Miss Allman would do her best for him. She was a good, caring woman. He could see that she cared about the children and young men under her care. Meanwhile, should he tell Shawna? He thought about it and decided not to. Shawna's pressure was up the last time she saw the doctor and he feared for her health. No, no one must know yet, not even Mammy. She might let it out and it would probably go back to Shawna and he dreaded the scene that would take place.

Meanwhile, he was wondering if any of the evening classes would take him in. He wondered if he could arrange to work in the days every working day and go to evening classes during the week. He could continue teaching the children on the weekends. He wanted to get his exam certificates and if possible go to Mico Teachers' College during the evenings. He had thought about it and every time he thought, he felt that it was something that he could do. He had to get his certificates and improve himself and his family and all the children around him. There were many private institutions offering classes to people like himself and classes started in September. He had to think of the cost too as Rhona would need uniforms and books and a small school fee if she succeeded in the Grade Six Achievement Test, and there were the other children to think about. He wanted to take the bulk of the burden off Shawna.

Shawna still sold trinkets downtown and sometimes A Butter felt guilty for having neglected her for so long. He knew now that he loved her and had always loved her, but had never been able to admit it and to make the commitment to a lifelong relationship. The children had come as a result of his own selfish needs with no consideration for her feelings. Now he really cared and respected her and he grew to love his children and those around him like he never thought he could.

Jason went to reform school in Stony Hill and Miss Allman kept in touch with him and relayed the information back to his father. A Butter was relieved that he was off the street and hoped against all hope that he would stay there for the two years that he was required to do so.

Miss Allman told him that there were some fights at the reform school and that Jason was often involved. She also said that he had sunk deeply into himself and had difficulty communicating with the other boys, but that the counselor there was working with him and reported some progress, albeit small at times. There was still hope. Two years was a long time for someone so young and he would change, she was sure of that.

Chapter 10

Shawna's blood pressure was up and she was irritable and miserable. A Butter went around with a long face. The children were too frightened to talk with her and only Mammy could soothe her. A Butter tried but got nowhere. For a while he went back to his old friends hoping that the domino games at the corner and the couple of beers were what he needed to help him but that only made things worse. He confided in Winner.

"She probably needs a holiday, some time away from everything even two days at a beach or river place where she can be alone or just the two of you. Try that. It will cost but funerals cost much more. Make Mammy take care of the children and the two of you go off somewhere to rest and relax for a while. Try the mineral baths like Milk River or Bath in St. Thomas. They good. Then you can lie in you bed and watch TV for two nights after the bath in the mineral water. Try it man. You working hard A Butter and summer is here so take off."

Winner hardly made so long a speech but this was one of them and A Butter went to his little room to think about it. He had a little put away now and he knew that Shawna had saved a bit and also threw 'partner' with her fellow higglers. Maybe they could work out something together. He wondered if he had any relatives in the countryside and once again he wished he knew his relatives but he knew nobody there as his mother seemed to have hidden him from them. What to do? He would ask for a Friday off and go on Friday and be back on Sunday. Back to work on Monday morning.

Then he remembered. June was approaching and it was Shawna's birthday month. She had told him that her birthday was the 3rd of June. He wanted to give her a birthday present.

He called the hotel at Milk River. He heard there was a bus that could take them from the city to May Pen and the taxis in May Pen would take them to the hotel; and he heard of the rates for two nights and three days. He could just manage to scrape it together without taking from Rhona's school fee and something of his own school fee if he decided to study again. He approached Shawna.

"Shawna. Mi want us to go weh for a little holiday, maybe down country. Maybe Milk River. Just mi and you for you birthday... make Mammy take care of the pickney them. What you say 'bout that?"

Shawna had been removing the yellow ackees from the red pods for dinner. She looked up at him.

"Milk River? Nuh expensive place that! You mad or what?"

"Mi call them and mi can manage it. You work too hard and you a worry too much. Shawna me care too much 'bout you to see you get a stroke. Come on man. Just mi and you. We can go."

Shawna looked up with a smile. "So you care 'bout me? Me never so sure 'bout that you know. So me can help with the cost? What 'bout Rhona school fee? And her books and uniform them if she pass the exam?"

"That all right. Please Shawna say yes."

"Mi would love to go with you. Mi going to get my draw from the partner next month so that will help with Rhona uniform them. A Butter you change. You know that? You change for the better. Jesus, thank you. I know that I sick and all of that and Milk River for two nights? Boy, I looking forward to it already."

She dropped the ackee pods and came to him and gave him a hug. A Butter held her close. It felt so good.

Plans had to be made to make sure that the children were fed and cared for in their absence. Mammy was in total agreement. Yes, both of them needed a break. She would cook the food and take care of the children while they were away. A Butter decided to pay her for the service she would provide and Shawna looked at him with wonder in her eyes. A Butter was changing fast. A former beggar now paying for a babysitter. It was remarkable.

A Butter had to ask someone at work to take his place at the bank that Friday and he would work another day in return. He was granted permission and that was that. They went downtown and boarded a bus that was available for the May Pen route but not before the three younger children clung to Shawna and cried. Shawna was almost having second thoughts about leaving them behind. But A Butter prevailed. They had already booked the room at Milk River. Shawna needed a break and he was going to give it to her.

They were off through the busy city streets and onto the road that led through the plains where the sugar cane fields swept the horizon on both sides of the road and then into lower Clarendon with its tiny houses and stark, dry countryside. The Milk River Hotel certainly didn't look like the place that they had expected. It was old and needed some repairs but they were settled in a fairly comfortable room with cable television and hot water in the taps. Shawna turned on the television set while A Butter brought up the luggage. He joined her and they watched CNN and then a movie before A Butter stirred and said he was going for his first bath. They were allowed three per day they had been told. Shawna stood up and decided to join him.

And what a bath it was. They opened the door to the bathhouse of which there were several and walked down the steps and into the water. It was warm and good, better even than a sea bath. They bathed and splashed and laughed while doing it. They were happy.

Dinner that night was excellent. They had oxtail and beans and lots of rice and peas and vegetables. Shawna remembered that she had to watch her diet so she didn't eat much of the rice and peas. They had hardly ever had the chance to eat so well.

"Next time we come I would love to bring the children. Just ask for two rooms," said Shawna when they were back in their room. "I hope they alright," she added.

"Mammy will take care of them," replied A Butter with a smile. "And Mammy would call the hotel if anything was wrong." Just then a shadow crossed his face as he remembered Jason. He had still not told Shawna anything about their eldest son. But telling her now would spoil everything for them. Shawna's face was alight with a kind of peace that he had not seen in a long time. They settled in for the night but not before they determined to take three baths the next day and watch television and just talk and enjoy each other's company. This was the first time that either of them had been a guest at a hotel.

If cheap Milk River was like this what were the huge, expensive hotels on the north coast like? What luxury were some people living in while they and so many others lived in squalor and deprivation?

But things were looking up for them now and both agreed that their children must enjoy the benefits that they, the parents, had never had. They chatted well into the night before they fell fast asleep with their hands wrapped around each other on the comfortable king-sized bed.

They awoke to the sound of choruses being sung and they put on clothes and went to the dining room where a group of guests and workers were clapping and singing religious choruses. They joined in. Then the Bible was read and breakfast was served. Another sumptuous meal of fish and festival with orange juice freshly squeezed and toast with coffee. They ate and went for the first bath for the day in the mineral water. It was lovely. Life could be so good at times.

Shawna and A Butter dressed afterwards and went for a walk. The landscape was dry as there was a drought but it was so different from the city. Hardly any noise and there were just some small shops along the road. The atmosphere was laid back and the people were willing to talk. They stepped into a shop and A Butter bought a beer and Shawna settled for a drink of spring water.

They chatted with the people in the shop and felt the welcoming nature of the country people. They heard about the crocodiles in the river and were warned not to move about too much at night. The water for the bath did not come from the river they were told, but from another source and they were relieved. Then after a nice chat and more greetings like "I hope we may never more be strangers", they went back to the hotel.

They took two more baths and had another great meal. Then to bed and the next day to an early morning prayer meeting, and another breakfast before they took their last bath and packed up to leave.

The weekend passed and they took a taxi to May Pen and a bus back to the city, and another one to Baker Street.

Between them, they had decided to try to rent a stall in the arcade for Shawna and that A Butter should pursue his education and if possible, try to become a teacher at the Mico evening school. They would try their best to rent maybe half of a house for the whole family on Baker Street and Shawna would contribute to the National Housing Trust so that they could borrow money at a low rate of interest and buy a house of their own in the future. A Butter was already contributing to the housing trust from his wages at his workplace. They were buzzing with hope and happiness and best of all, they had grown to know each other better and love each other more.

It had been a great weekend. Shawna was much better and they realized how important a real holiday away from everything was. Now they understood the importance of a tourist destination. Poorer Jamaicans hardly took holidays off as they had done, only the wealthy did that. They arrived home happy and relaxed and were greeted by Mammy and the children. Shawna said that it was the best birthday present she had ever had.

Chapter 11

That Sunday night after the trip to Milk River, A Butter took pen and paper and began to write a poem. This time it flowed. This time the words came where they should and he had very little difficulty putting it onto paper. It was a long poem and he sat in bed and read it aloud. He knew it was not finished yet. It needed work. It needed him to edit it and make it perfect. That took time. He called the poem *Escape into Love* and smiled as he put the title at the top of the page. He was beginning to write again. It didn't matter now if no one heard him recite it, it was enough that he was writing again after all this time when his mind had been dry and his pen empty of inspiration.

A Butter felt peaceful and happy. He went to work on Monday morning with a song lilting on his lips and a broad smile on his face. He did his morning and evening shifts and went to a cook shop that evening. He wanted to spare Shawna of the need to cook. He bought jerk chicken and rice. He went home, changed from his uniform and went to Shawna's place. Sean ran to him and hugged him around his waist.

"Come Daddy, I have something to show you. I paint a picture and Mama say it look good."

Sean ran towards the room that they all occupied with Shawna and came running back with his painting. It was a painting of the yard with the garbage tin in the centre and some chickens pecking at dirt. There was the sun in the sky and white clouds in the background. It was a child's painting but A Butter felt a burst of pride. It was really good for a five-year old to draw like that.

A Butter lifted his son as Rhona took the food from him. A Butter hugged Sean and all the other children came for their hugs. It was the first time that A Butter had really hugged his children.

Mammy came to the door and smiled at the family. A Butter burst into laughter and said to her, "Shawna come yet?"

"Not yet. She tell me you trying to get a stall at the arcade for her. A Butter a really proud of you. You is a real family man now. You know that?"

"Mammy I never know it was so sweet. After all these years mi just a learn how to live."

"A telling you. You live and you learn. That's life. Better late than never," said Mammy.

"Me carry some jerk chicken and some rice and peas."

"When Shawna come, she will share it," answered Mammy, shepherding Roly away from the food package. Roly loved his food.

"Shawna tell me you enjoy Milk River," said Mammy. "You must carry the children for a day trip one day."

"Milk River nice. But you would have to come with us you know Mammy. You is family you know."

"A Butter you change for true. You hear anything about Jason?"

A cloud passed over A Butter's face. He no longer wanted to lie but he had to, this time.

"Not a thing. Jason disappear. Mammy I wish him would just come home, just come back. That is all I hope for now."

"We can only pray. The good Lord will take care of him if we just pray," replied Mammy who was a regular churchgoer. She sang in the choir at the Church of God down the road.

"Mmmhm," said A Butter who had not gone to church in years. He felt that he had to learn to really pray. Sometimes he muttered a prayer to God but he wondered if God really heard him. Church had never meant much to him as a child.

"Daddy, Mama look better," observed Rhona. "You too," she added.

A Butter stayed till Shawna came home and the family ate one of their favourite meals which they shared with Mammy and her granddaughter Marie. It was a jolly evening and late that night as the moon shone over the ramshackle yard, Mammy told them an Anancy story. Brer Tiger was fooled as he always was by the clever Anancy. The children went to bed full of the story and family contentment.

Shawna and A Butter chatted well into the night with Mammy who was full of advice. But nobody mentioned Jason again although he occupied their minds. A Butter made his way back to 10 Baker Street and fell asleep the instant he hit the bed. That night he dreamt of Miss Allman. Miss Allman looked at him and there was concern written all over her face. A Butter was sweating when he woke up early the next morning to hear a loud knocking on his door. He got up and opened the door. It was his friend Winner and he had a note in his hand.

"For you," said Winner handing him the note. "Morning. You alright? You look kind of sick."

"Mi alright for now. Who this from?" asked A Butter pulling open the envelope.

"Mi nuh know. Gold Teeth say to give you. Him get it from a man in Stony Hill."

A Butter frowned. Jason's reform school was located in Stony Hill. He started to read and as he read he turned pale.

"You alright man?" asked Winner.

"Is alright Winner. Everything alright," answered A Butter.

"Mi have to go now. See you then," said Winner. "Long time you nuh come pon de corner. What happen?"

"Family business." A Butter could barely answer the friend he had had for so many years.

The letter in his hand spoke volumes. Winner looked at him then turned and left the yard. He was concerned about A Butter.

A Butter sat on the bed and read the letter again. Jason wrote:

Look beggar man. Is you why the boy them here calling me beggar boy cause you always a beg on the street. You leave my mother alone. She too good for you. When I get out of this place I going to see to it that you two separate. I don't want you to give her more children. Is five you give her already. You leave her alone you hear me. Or is murder when I get out of here.

A Butter put the letter on the bed beside him and put his face in his hands. So Jason was thinking of killing him. His own son was going to commit murder if he didn't leave Shawna alone.

A Butter prayed. "Dear God, help me. I don't know what to do now. I love Shawna and I can't leave her now. Please tell me what to do."

He wiped his tears and then stood up resolute. This was a letter from a child, his child. He, A Butter, was a big man. Why should he fear a letter from a child? A Butter hid the letter among some books and dressed quickly. He had to go to work. He resolved not to tell Shawna or anyone about the threat. Shawna would probably have a stroke and he didn't want the news to go around that Jason was a potential murderer. The police, should he tell them? He would decide later. Now he had to go to work. He dared not be late.

A Butter made a hasty stop at the nearest cook shop and ate a slice of bread and drank a cup of tea. Then he made his way to the bus stop but for the first time in many months, he felt real fear.

Chapter 12

A Butter went to work but his heart was not in it. He wondered how he would get through the day. An elderly customer at the bank who he saw almost every week looked at him and smiled. "Cheer up man. You look sick, you alright?" she asked.

A Butter smiled wanly back at her. At least someone cared, even though it was a stranger.

"Look like the flu taking me," he answered.

"When you go home, drink a tot of white rum and wrap up tight in a blanket. Nothing beat the flu like that."

"Alright Mam," answered A Butter. "I will try it tonight", and he opened the door to let the caring customer out.

A Butter was glad when his shift was over and he could walk home. As he walked down the busy street avoiding the vendors and the people on the sidewalk, he resolved that he was going to make things so right between his family and himself that Jason would be surprised when he came home from reform school and be happy with what he had done. He would hide the letter. No one else would see it.

He wondered if he should visit Jason but decided against it. Jason was apparently not happy at the school because of the name calling. Beggar boy. How did they know that he, A Butter, used to beg on the street? Life was so strange and the world was small. Somebody knew and spread that rumour about his son. But then Jason had chosen to be a beggar boy too until Miss Allman took him off the street. Where was the difference between them?

When he arrived home he stripped himself of his uniform and put on other clothes. He had no white rum in the house, that was expensive. He would go and see the children and help them with their reading. It was now approaching the summer holidays and they had gone to the library the evening before. He also decided to check out the schools for evening classes. He would make sure he had enough money to pay the first term's fee. Jason's letter caused him to want to take action faster. It did not deter him from improving his family and himself.

"Daddy, Daddy come!" shouted   Sean and he walked into the yard.

A Butter laughed happily as he picked up the child and held him close. "You mother come home yet?" he asked Sean.

"No Daddy. You want to see me drawing? Is you and Mama I draw."

"Alright go for it," replied A Butter, putting him down. The child ran into the room and came back with a sheet of drawing paper. The other children came from around the side of the house.

A Butter took the paper and looked at it. The five-year old had drawn a picture of himself and Shawna hugging each other. And at the bottom he had written the words, *Love, Mama and Daddy*. It was so hard not to cry.

A Butter held him close and kissed him on his cheek. The other children came around for their kisses and

Shawna came through the corrugated iron gate and stood watching the scene. Her face was wearing a wide smile. "At last," she muttered to herself. "At last."

A Butter turned and saw her. They stood looking at each other for a long time and then she ran into his arms. It was a happy family that Mammy came to her own doorway to see. She too was smiling.

"Come," said A Butter to Shawna. "We have to plan. The family can't live apart like this. Me in one house and you and the pickney them in another house, we have to find a place where we can all live with one another like one united family."

Mammy left the verandah, came into the yard and took over. "Miss Kelly have her half of a house for rent. Miss Kelly at 22 Baker Street. She tell me that last week. You would share the kitchen with her but you have your own bathroom. You want me to talk to her? The rent not too high. You can manage it now that A Butter in a job and all."

"Yow!" A Butter punched the air with his fists. "Mammy you have the solution to every problem. Talk to Miss Kelly for me please, and find out if we can move in next month."

"We have to give notice to these landlords," cautioned Shawna.

"Oh come on man, they will find tenant easy, easy," said A Butter.

"We going to be a real family now," said Rhona. "And Jason not here to see us. I wonder where him is. Jason always wanted us to be together. Him always cry that Daddy not here. And now that Daddy is here him not here."

The child's lament cast a shadow over everything. Shawna put her hands to her face and A Butter put his arm around her. Then they all walked back into the one room.

"We have to get you that stall in the arcade downtown," said A Butter to Shawna. "I just wondering who to ask."

"The KSAC," answered Shawna. "But we have to get it

stocked. Mi have to wait till I get another draw from mi partner then I can maybe get to stock it. I want to sell things that nobody else sell so that I can get the market."

"One thing you can do when our expenses ease up is join the credit union. They will lend money at low rates of interest. But I really want to start the CXC classes come September. I feel that I can do it. Now is the chance. Now is the time. I don't want to wait till a too old and gray," A Butter said, musing as he sat and looked at the one hanging light bulb.

"I would be so proud if you could do that and then go to Mico evening school to become a teacher."

"Daddy teach me so good. All of us understand the lesson when him teach. I want my Daddy to be a teacher," said Rhona.

It was getting dark and that night Mammy cooked for them and they all ate together. She was all right financially but she was lonely and loved Shawna, A Butter and their children. She was not close to the other tenants in the yard. A Butter's family was like her own adopted family. She knew Miss Kelly would say yes and they were just across the road. She would pop in and see them every day.

On the way back to his room A Butter thought of Jason and wondered how he could get him back in the family unit. He wondered if Miss Allman would help him and determined to ask her as soon as his day off came again. That night the only thought that dulled his happiness was the thought of his eldest son in reform school and the letter that Jason had written to him.

Jason's plight was the only cloud in his sky now and he was determined to remove it before it became a storm. He would continue to give Miss Allman money to send things for Jason if she could get in touch with the matron at the reform school. He hadn't given anything much since the boy went to the school. He didn't want her to think that he had abandoned his son. He would call Miss Allman the next day from his workplace. He prayed that all would be well.

Later that month the Grade Six Achievement Test results came out. Rhona had passed for a good high school. There was jubilation in the family and all over Baker Street. A Butter was especially proud knowing that he had helped her to do well. More children flocked to the Sunday afternoon classes that he had started.

Then Shawna dropped what was to him a bomb. Jason was now fifteen. His birthday was in the month of July. A Butter had forgotten that. His first son was growing up. A Butter, a tall man himself, wondered just how tall Jason had grown. Although expenses were up A Butter resolved to send a special present to Jason for his birthday which was the fourteenth of July.

He asked Miss Allman to buy a small cake and take it for him. He gave her some money and Miss Allman agreed and said that she would buy a candle or two for him and she would drive up and celebrate with the other boys at the reform school. First she had to get permission from the matron whom she knew well, but she still would not tell Jason who sent it.

It was a lighthearted A Butter who left the YMCA building and walked to the bus stop that Saturday evening. He had the gut feeling that everything was going to be alright in the end.

He just hoped that the feeling would be true. A Butter had become a perennial optimist.

He was so happy now that he entered the poem *Escape into Love* that he had written in the Jamaica Cultural Development Commission creative writing competition. He had worked hard on the poem and he had written two others which were shorter. They were more of an older style of poetry like some that he had learnt at school. A Butter held his breath as he took the three typed copies of each, and entered them under a pseudonym. He filled out the application form and handed them in at the commission's headquarters. He would have to wait for some months before he knew the results. Whatever it was, he was beginning to write again.

Chapter 13

The next few days went by like a breeze. He went to work and did his job to the best of his ability. The hours were long and at times tedious, but he had time to think and plan. Sometimes he looked longingly at the men and women who were able to leave the bank with lots of cash in their pockets or handbags. But the time when he might have begged or grabbed a bag were behind him now. He had his honour to preserve and protect, and he could not help remembering that that was the reason for Jason's seeming rejection of him. He had been a beggar and a kind of petty thief. Yes, he had grabbed a bag or two and also picked a few pockets when his own pocket was empty and his stomach growled. But that was behind him. He had never had to go to reform school as a child nor had he gone to prison, and he did not have a police record. He was free of all of that. Life had changed for him even though there had been no defining moment that he could state when it had changed. It had been gradual and the new found freedom from petty crime that he felt made him want to stay that way.

The night before his next day off he went to eat dinner at the children's place. Shawna had cooked a meal of jerk chicken back and rice.

"We can move into the house at number 22 next week," she told him. "But is three rooms and we have to furnish it. I have the two beds and you have one. We also have the dinette set for the living room and you have a few chairs and the bookcase. That will do for the time being. A Butter we moving up now."

A Butter chewed a piece of chicken bone and smiled though his mouth was full. "You know mi just understanding family life. Mi never have a father and mi never really appreciate mi mother and all she do for mi when she was around. But now, I know family good, it really sweet. And every day mi love mi family more. Is like everything change since you sick. Like God a show mi things even though mi can't tell when last mi go to church and them things there."

It was a long speech for A Butter. He finished chewing the bone and sat still for a while. Shawna smiled at him as the children looked on with wide open eyes. They had never heard their father talk like that before.

"Maybe I get sick for that purpose you know. You never can tell where it can all lead. Everything happen for a reason, my guardian always tell me that," said Shawna.

"If you can really use the experience well," said Mammy coming through the open door. She had been standing there, listening.

"Aye Mammy. You hear what we all saying," said Shawna smiling at her.

"I hear it good," quipped Mammy. "And I like what I hear. I have a proposal to put to you A Butter."

"Yes Mam," answered A Butter, wondering what it was.

"Supposing I pay your daughter school fee and give her pocket money, you will work hard and get through your studies just for everybody, mi included? We is all one family now. All I have here is mi granddaughter and I feel like all of you is mi family now. I know that you proud and thing but is something I want to do to feel needed. I need all of you and I want to feel like you need me too especially now that you moving out next week. Please don't say no. I want to do this. I know it hard with more rent to pay and Rhona going to the high school uptown. But I want to do it. Please."

Shawna started to cry and A Butter sat there with his mouth wide open.

"Mammy, you would do that for me? For me who used to be a..." he never finished the sentence cause Mammy came around and hugged him.

"I want you to forget the past. The time is now. I want the family to grow into a model family. You nuh hear the children calling you Mr. Butterfield? You teach them and you is Mr. Butterfield to them now so what? You will let me do it?"

"I tell you what. Let me teach you granddaughter for her GSAT. I can do it Sundays when she come from church. That all right with you?" asked A Butter.

"If it all right with mi? Then you know what you saying? Teach mi granddaughter and the school fee and pocket money for Rhona will be my compensation. Good, that settled now."

"I will sit up nights. I will work hard. Mammy, you good. Thank you."

The family moved into the house at 22 Baker Street the following week and A Butter and Shawna were so happy as were the children. The first month's rent was paid and the family members pitched in to make the place look really good. Shawna bought curtains for the windows and cushions for the chairs and said to A Butter that Rhona can bring her friend's home now, she had no reason to feel ashamed.

August rolled in. The children were home from school and Mammy took care of them while Shawna and A Butter went to work. The children played every day but went to their father for lessons in the nights and on Sunday evenings after church.

Chapter 14

August 12th was A Butter's birthday and Shawna and Mammy decided to celebrate it with him. Mammy approached him on the first weekend of August month.

"A Butter. I hear that your birthday coming up, what you going to do about it?"

"Do about it? Mi never do anything 'bout mi birthday before?" A Butter sounded surprised.

"What about us going to Port Royal? Just a trip, me, you and Shawna and the pickney them."

"But Mammy, the expense. Mi can't afford it!"

"Shawna and me not asking you to do anything. We have it all planned. Me getting a small mini bus and we all going to Port Royal for a walk around the place and then get a fish meal. They sell good fish out there; you know and me know you love fish," answered Mammy quietly.

"Mammy you would do that for me? You and Shawna? Mi never celebrate mi birthday before."

"Well you going to do it now," answered Mammy firmly. "So no excuses. We going on Saturday next week so cancel all you other plans. Don't disappoint us. We just saying thank you and we all love you like how you love us. Alright?"

A Butter had gone to Port Royal on a school trip many years before. He remembered the Palisadoes Road and the sea on both sides of the road and Fort Charles. He remembered the Giddy house. He knew that his children had never been much outside of the city and its environs. He knew he was already looking forward to it.

A Butter and the children prepared for the journey as though they were taking a plane to go off the island. They were so excited. A Butter scarcely knew how he got through the week. That Saturday morning, he dressed in his best holiday clothes and helped Shawna with the children. Mammy turned up with little Marie in tow. They were ready long before the driver with the minibus came up the road and they all piled in. Sean had his latest drawing book. He wanted to draw and paint a picture of Port Royal.

The minibus accommodated the family and they were all seated and ready to move. The driver smiled at them and jumped into his seat. They were off. Through the city streets and down Windward Road past the cement factory and onto the narrow strip of road between the blue-green Caribbean Sea. It was getting hot in the minibus but the children looked wide-eyed at the scenery around them. They were excited to say the least.

The driver pointed out the way to the airport and the family paused for a moment to watch a plane take off.

"I wonder if I will ever take a plane somewhere?" Roly wondered aloud. "Or if I will ever be able to fix one if it broke down?"

"Roly only thinks of fixing things that break down," observed Julie.

"Just like you only think of fixing food in the kitchen," countered Roly.

"Ok children no fuss now. This is a holiday," said Shawna sternly and things were quiet for a while till the bus rode smoothly into the little town of Port Royal and they all stepped out to view the scene.

It was so quiet and laid back with a few people going about their business and the sea lapping the shore in the distance.

"This was once the wickedest city in the world?" Rhona wondered out loud as she looked around. "It's so quiet now. Maybe the earthquake did its job well."

They looked around and saw the police training school, the fort on the other side of the street and the tumble of houses that lined the narrow streets. *It was quaint*, A Butter thought. "Yes quaint is the word to describe this place," he voiced aloud.

"Quaint? I will look up that word," said Rhona quietly to herself.

"Come see the Giddy House. Children love that," said the driver. And he led the way to a strange looking house among the many places they wanted to see.

"Step inside," he said as they approached the strange place. The children went in and felt like falling. The floor of the small building felt like they were one side up. Sean ran out.

"I feel dizzy," he said, holding on to his mother who held him close. She was laughing as the others came trooping out of the house and were back on solid ground.

"What caused that?" asked Roly.

"The earthquake of 1692," said A Butter. "It destroyed half the town which sank under the sea and there are people who dive under to see that remains of the place down there."

"I want to learn to swim and dive," said Roly. "So I can go and see."

"Many people died in that earthquake but there is a

story of a man called Lewis Galdy who was covered up under the earth and came out again. He lived after the earthquake to tell the tale." A Butter was teaching now. He remembered his history.

"Why were they so wicked?" asked Rhona.

"Money the buccaneers brought in," said A Butter who was pleased to be able to answer these questions.

"Buccaneers?" asked Sean who was holding his drawing book in his hand as though he wanted to draw all of Port Royal.

"They were pirates who raided places that the Spaniards owned and brought back money and jewels and lots of gold and silver. I tell you what, we will read about it all later. I will borrow a book from the library and we will all read. Meanwhile, fish Mammy, I am hungry. You promised fish dinners," said A Butter, rubbing his stomach. He too felt the need to read up on Port Royal. He felt that his history was really a bit rusty now after all these years.

They made their way to a tiny restaurant and all found seats. There were other patrons there and some were eating and others waiting patiently. The food smelled so good it made Roly's mouth water. He shifted impatiently about while Shawna and Mammy made the orders. They ordered fish and festival and they would wash that down with a good tropical fruit punch.

When the food came, they all dipped in and Shawna had to remind them that overeating could make them sick. If they wanted, they could take some of the food home with them. She asked for doggie bags as the food was too much for little Sean and Marie, and they all pitched in to give up some of their lunch. It would serve them all that night.

After eating Mammy started a song going. She sang happy birthday to A Butter and the others joined in. The other patrons also sang and somebody hollered, "Speech, Speech, whose birthday is it?"

A Butter stood and blushed.

"It's mine," he said simply. "I just want to thank my children's mother and Mammy and the children you see here for a wonderful birthday. I thoroughly enjoyed it. Thanks Shawna and Mammy for arranging this and thank you all for what you all do to make me happy."

Then came the applause. A Butter sat down confused and happy. He had never really made a speech before.

After the meal they went to explore Fort Charles and A Butter decided to read up about it in order to tell the children more. It was about three in the afternoon that they left the little city that was more like a tiny village and headed home. It was a day to remember all their lives. A Butter knew he would cherish that day all his days as it was the first time anyone had helped him to celebrate his birthday.

Chapter 15

A Butter was now thirty-six years old. He felt old but determined to see the training he needed through. He felt that he could excel as a teacher and he felt the satisfaction that every teacher feels when the students learnt and understood.

The new place meant a new life too as they fixed it up and they were a real family now with all of them living in the same house. Miss Kelly was an elderly lady who was kind and understanding to the children even when they made noise playing in the backyard. She told A Butter that she would be grateful if he and the children could help her to plant a vegetable garden as there was space for this.

A Butter worked on that on Saturday afternoons and soon ploughed the place with a machete and hoe. The children helped to clear away the rubbish from the weeds and Rhona decided to plant flowers in the front of the house where there was also space. Miss Kelly was keen on the garden saying that she had never been able to afford the help to plant one. A Butter planted cabbages and callaloo and carrots, and Rhona planted a bougainvillea plant and some hibiscus flowers to form a hedge. The children made sure that they watered the plants and kept the plots clean from weeds.

The children read a lot of books from the library and A Butter still taught the neighbourhood children on weekends. He paid special attention to Marie and saw that she loved to read books about animals so he made her borrow those from the library and he explained some of the stories that she couldn't understand. Mammy was pleased with her progress and more and more children joined the classes. A Butter was often asked what he charged for the lessons and he said, "Nothing, I just want the children to learn, that is all I ask. It gives me enough joy to do it and that is payment enough."

Summer holidays ended and as September began, A Butter found an evening class with a good reputation and began his classes in the nights. Rhona started out at her new school and came home that first evening with her eyes full of stars.

"Mama I going to learn" was all she said before she sat at the table to begin her homework. The other children saw how happy she was and resolved to learn too at the primary school they attended and to try hard to go to one of the good high schools. After Rhona's homework, the family was regaled with news of the new school, the teachers for every subject and the children in her class. She had already made one friend and hoped to be friends with some others. She spoke of the food at the canteen and the games that they would play. She wanted to play netball as she had at her old school and she loved her English teacher more than all the others. A Butter wondered if he had fathered a writer like himself.

That night A Butter sat and wrote a poem to celebrate his new status. He was a responsible father and he had a job. He was a student again and the words were flowing now. He no longer considered himself a sufferer but someone on the way to success. He too resolved to work hard. He wanted to be an example to his children.

Shawna had applied to the KSAC for the stall in the arcade and was awaiting a reply. She determined to sell costume jewelry and other accessories like handbags, hats and some cosmetics. She had noticed that were no stalls in the arcade that sold those things and she remembered how well she had done just selling trinkets from a box. She felt that there was a market for those goods and later she would even try fancy underwear for both men and women.

She decided to save to go overseas to Panama or Curacao to buy things in bulk but she would have to wait until she had saved enough before she could make the trip. Meanwhile, she was doing her best to keep well and went to the clinic at the hospital on a regular basis. She took her medication every day and tried to eat right all the time.

Julie cooked meals sometimes when her mother was still downtown and she cooked well in spite of her age. Roly excelled at math in school and Sean was forever drawing things in the drawing books his father gave him. In short, it was a united family except for one thing, the absent Jason. Shawna hardly spoke about him now but there was a look of sadness in her eyes as she looked at her growing family, especially after a meal when they all sat around the dinette set in the little living room. A Butter would sigh and wish his son was there with them. But he knew that Jason would be at the reform school for two years at least, and he had learnt from Miss Allman that he was doing craft work and carpentry and some CXC subjects. He was settling she told him when he asked her on the telephone at work. Could he tell Shawna all what was going on? He often wondered but he was afraid she would break down as being at reform school meant to many people that your child was tantamount to being called a criminal. He decided against it. He would wait and see what would happen when he was released. Meanwhile life went on at 22 Baker Street with A Butter teaching and learning and also earning. He had two days off, Saturday and Sunday and he taught the children from Baker Street for two hours on each of those days now. Many of his nights were spent studying after hours on the little porch outside the living room where the boys slept. He would do his exams in May. Meanwhile he applied for a place at the Mico Teachers' College evening school. He was determined to succeed.

He wrote poems now and again whenever he felt the urge and as he read more, he was delighted to see that his ideas were flowing better and easier. He no longer felt that a block was hindering him from expressing himself. He decided to try short story writing and did his first short story on the yellow writing pad. He would have to get it typed if he was to send it in to the newspapers. He had no typewriter nor could he type. He had to learn to do that if he was going to be a writer of note.

One night after studying he sat back in the chair and marveled at how much had happened in so short a time. It was not so long ago that he put on old clothes, and an old crepe sole shoes with the holes showing through and begged on the streets. He remembered picking pockets and wondered now how he had never been caught at it except for the one time he had been beaten by onlookers. He remembered the hunger he had often felt and his shameless dependence on Shawna for a few dollars in order to eat and how she had never told him no. He hung his head in shame as he remembered this and he was happy that his life had changed. He looked at the darkened sky and saw the stars. There was no moon that night. A Butter closed his eyes and thought of the wonder of everything and the vastness of space that he had often read about. He was so small, so insignificant, yet he was an important part of it and the universe was evolving as it should. A Butter smiled, got up and made his way back to his bed.

Life and much of it still lay ahead of him.

Chapter 16

One morning, just as A Butter was going out the front door to go to work, Winner entered the yard and handed him an envelope. A Butter looked at the writing on the envelope. He knew that it was Jason again. A Butter sighed.

"Thanks," he said to Winner. "Who gave it to you?"

"Gold Teeth give it to Blacka and Blacka ask me to give you. You not going to read it?"

"Not now, when I go to work," answered A Butter. His heart was beating fiercely and he felt a bit of anger growing in him. Winner patted him on the back.

"Cheer up man. Nothing can be so bad that yuh face look so down," said Winner.

"You nuh know Winner," said A Butter. "When you feel peace and safety a sudden destruction."

"Is so life go. Sometimes you up, sometimes you down. But when you up it really sweet. So go on to work and let me know if I can help, alright?"

"Alright. Thanks," replied A Butter as he arrived at the

bus stop. He was happy that he was out of the house and that Shawna didn't know about the letters. This was the second one now. What did it say? His bus came and he climbed the steps and sat in a seat at the back. Winner was a close friend but he could never share this with him or anyone, except perhaps Miss Allman. Yes, he would speak to Miss Allman if the letter was another threat to him. He was glad for the company of strangers on the bus and looked around at them as they all sat there in the early morning, all going somewhere, school, workplaces, all showing signs of tiredness even though this was the morning hour and they had most likely slept the night through.

Life was difficult for a working man and for the women who worked tirelessly at home and at work. Many of the women in the bus were domestic helpers who had to leave their own children to go to work in some rich man's palace uptown. But A Butter was too busy now to lament the plight of the working class. He had been worse off than they were now. That was what this letter was all about. He had been a beggar, a pickpocket and a negligent father, and this letter in his pocket attested to all that he had been. Things were changing for him and he could eat without pretending to be blind or lame. He had a baby mother who loved him in spite of everything and children who clung to him when he went home. He had his books to study from and he was teaching the youth in the area around him and he was happy now. What did this letter say? He decided to read it at work before the bank opened its doors to the public.

He arrived early at the bank and looked around, there was no one else there. He sat in a corner near the door and opened the envelope. The letter fell out. With a fast beating heart, he picked it up, opened it and started to read. His heart sank as though into his shoes.

Daddy, I been in this place for months now and not one of you even ask where I am. It show that you nuh care 'bout me. Neither you nor mama care if I am dead or alive. Strangers helping me and not a word from you. I can't curse Mama cause she sick, but you nuh business with me or any of the children that you give her. I know that you don't have it but you could ask.

Jason

No, Jason did not know that he, A Butter was the stranger. He had told Miss Allman never to tell and this was the result. What was he to do? He wanted the boy to know that he cared deeply about him, but was Jason hating him that much? He read the letter again and knew that the teen just wanted to know that his father and mother cared about him. He had to see Miss Allman and ask her what she thought. He would call her on the phone at work and arrange a meeting. It would be difficult as his next day off was the following week and Miss Allman didn't work on some weekends. In the evenings he went to classes and he dared not miss a class.

The other security guards came and he stood and folded the letter, put it in the envelope then into his pocket and went to work. The hours were long but he was making a living. The money was small to cope with all the responsibilities that he faced but he was happy to have a job. It meant so much. Later, at lunchtime, he arranged to see Miss Allman the following Saturday. She was going to be at the YMCA then. Today was Tuesday and it seemed a long time to wait but wait he would.

The days seemed to stretch but Saturday came at last and after teaching his little group in the morning, A Butter took the bus to the YMCA.

There were many children in the swimming pool and the

grounds were full of people. Miss Allman was in her office waiting and he went in to her with the letter in his hand.

"Morning Miss Allman," he said and silently handed her the letter to read.

She took it from him and quietly read it, then she looked up and smiled at him.

"Now is the time to tell him everything. Have you told his mother about all you have been doing? Because you have been doing a lot."

"No Miss Allman 'cause I am afraid that she'll get a stroke. She has high blood pressure and she is diabetic too. She worries a lot about him and with him in a reform school it looks as though he is a criminal. That's why I don't tell her."

"Tell her but don't show her the letter yet. I am going to see what I can do to get you to him or him to you. I tell you what, what about a family reunion? I could get leave to take him to you with your whole family there and I would tell him in front of everybody, all that you have done for him. I tell you what, don't say a word to his mother just leave it to me. Oh boy I am looking forward to this. What is your address? I could pick him up and take him to you one Sunday. Alright? I will call you. I have your work number. Just you wait and see. I really admire you Mr. Butterfield. So what's up? What have you been doing with yourself?"

A Butter told her of the move to the house at 22 Baker Street, his classes at the evening school, his classes in his yard with the children, and his ambition to become a teacher. He told her of Rhona at her new school, Shawna getting a stall in the arcade later on and the other children's ambition and hard work. He told her of Mammy and how she looked after the children sometimes for them and how good she was to Rhona.

Miss Allman smiled. "All good news to tell your son Jason. I will try to get him to come with me if the matron will agree, alright? I will call you and tell you the date and time. A Sunday evening is best for me as I attend church on a Sunday morning. I hope Jason will have good news to tell you too. Matron tells me that they do the CXC exams there and they all learn a skill. Don't worry, it will all work out I tell you, it will."

Miss Allman smiled at him and shook his hand. A Butter rose and smiled through tears. Jason was coming home to see them.

"Thanks Miss Allman. I really don't know how to thank you."

"Thank God," she said, as he emotionally fled through the door.

Chapter 17

"Shawna, I have something to tell you," said A Butter as he sat up in bed the Saturday morning.

"This sounds serious. What happen?" asked Shawna with alarm in her voice. A Butter rarely spoke like this.

"Jason," said A Butter simply.

"What happen? Him dead?" Shawna was about to scream.

"No, no, him nuh dead. Him alright. Him coming to see us tomorrow."

"Where him was? You know all this time and you nuh tell me? A Butter him is mi pickney! Him coming home at last?" Tears were flowing. Shawna was crying now. "Tell me," she said.

A Butter told her everything. When he told her that Jason had used a knife and cut a child, he had to hold Shawna tight because she was sobbing.

"Shhh," he said. "You waking the children. Mi nuh want them to know. Mi want it to be a surprise. Tell Mammy though cause mi want her to help you to cook curry goat and rice and them things there."

"Who is this Miss Allman?" asked Shawna.

"She work at the YMCA. She help plenty people. She take the boys them off the street and she teach them skills," replied A Butter.

Shawna was no longer crying. She jumped from the bed and put on her clothes. She went to the bathroom to wash her face and she was as busy as a bee for the entire morning. She scrubbed the floor and she cleaned every room. She put on the best sheets on the beds and she fixed breakfast and lunch. She rushed over to Mammy and told her the news. The children were alarmed.

"Daddy what happen to Mama?" asked Julie.

"Nuh worry, she alright," answered A Butter.

He too was a bit frightened at the burst of activity. Shawna could get stroke so he insisted that she take her medication that night and on Sunday morning. He bought the goat meat and stored it in Mammy's fridge. He got rice from the shop at the corner and vegetables from the market. Everything was alright now and Mammy shared in the excitement. It was hard to keep the secret from the children, who wondered if it was somebody's birthday.

The children went to Sunday school that morning and A Butter went for the first time in years to the service. Mammy and Shawna stayed home to cook the food and get everything ready. Miss Allman had said she would be there by two o'clock that afternoon so A Butter got the children home from church in time, and he had already cancelled his class with the students for the day. Rhona, Julie, Sean and Roly looked on wide-eyed as the little company sat on the verandah and waited. Miss Allman was just a little late, ten minutes in fact. The white Toyota Corolla drove up and stopped. A Butter jumped up and ran to the gate to open it. He was a bit nervous, so too was Shawna.

Miss Allman came out of the car. Her movements were a bit slow as she was an elderly lady. The young man sitting in the front seat of the car was trimmed and clean. He looked a bit bewildered. This was Baker Street but this was not number 10 or number 26 where his parents lived. Miss Kelly came around to the passenger seat and opened the door. Jason, in new clothes and pair of new sneakers came out slowly. Rhona screamed and ran to him. Shawna started to cry. Mammy stood with folded hands and watched with a smile on her face. Julie jumped up and down. Sean ran inside to get his latest painting. Roly laughed loud and long and A Butter looked at his son with a look of sheer love on his face. He was silent as a mouse.

Jason turned to Miss Allman as if to say, why have you done this? Miss Allman just nodded and said quietly, "You have a loving family Jason, they all live together now."

"But, but how? Mi father was a beggar and a pick pocket. How come them come to live here together? Mi nuh understand," said Jason as he ignored Rhona's efforts to hug him.

"Not anymore," replied Miss Allman. "He has a good job now and he is studying again. He wants to be a teacher."

"Teacher? My father?" asked the still puzzled Jason.

"Yes Jason and him can teach good. Is him help me pass the GSAT and me going to the high school uptown and him teaching everybody on Baker Street now. Jason, you come home? Me glad to see you. Where you was?" Rhona was happy.

Suddenly Shawna was off the steps and in Jason's arms and Sean clamored to show him his painting. Roly hugged Jason from behind and Mammy cried and Miss Allman stood and watched. A Butter just observed it all with a bemused smile on his face.

Then Shawna took over and led the family into the house and onto the verandah. Mammy got her hugs then and A Butter came onto the verandah and sat on a chair. He seemed not to know how to greet Jason. He just looked at him.

"Jason," said Miss Allman as she took over now. "You see those clothes you have on and that money and things I gave you all the time over the past months that you have been in reform school and before? They came from Mr. Butterfield here, your father. He came to me with your photograph and asked me to find you on the street and take you into the YMCA. He came to see me time and time again to see your progress, and he has been in touch with me for many months now. So people do care about you. He never told anyone that he knew where you were. He just did what he could. And now you are here. He loves you very much and he wants to hug you too. So go over and hug him. He is a changed man now. Go on, hug him."

Jason got up and went to his father who held him close for what seemed like ages. Then A Butter looked at Jason's face which was bathed in tears. "You alright?" he asked Jason.

"Daddy, mi sorry. Mi never know." Jason sobbed.

"Is alright. You know now. That is all I want, Jason you know now."

Then Mammy took over. "Come let we eat," she said as she led the company into the tiny room and seated Jason, his father, Miss Allman and Shawna on the four chairs around the dinette set, and the others on the bed in the corner where the boys slept. They ate the curried goat and rice with the shredded cabbage and sliced tomatoes which they washed down with carrot juice. It was a comfortable silence in the room and they all ate with enjoyment for the food was good.

Jason told them that he was going to do three subjects in CXC the following year and that he was interested in carpentry and craftwork, and that he was learning well in the reform school. The boys had stopped calling him names and he had friends now. He no longer felt the need to fight anyone. He would finish reform school the following

August and he was looking forward to coming home now that so much had changed. He was happy for his father and he was glad that his mother was keeping well and that she was getting the stall in the arcade. He wanted Rhona to do well and Julie and Roly to pursue their dreams. Then he hugged little Sean and looked at the painting that he had been dying to show him. "It's good," A Butter said as he looked at the painting of a hibiscus flower. Sean blushed with joy.

Jason left with Miss Allman at six o'clock that evening. He was quiet but full of inner peace. Miss Allman shook all the hands around and was told thank you by everyone. She said she only did what she wanted to do and what she had to do considering the circumstances.

A Butter was happiest of all. He had his son back. He had his family with him and they were full of gladness. That night after all else had gone to bed, A Butter sat on the verandah and looked at the stars. They were so far away yet he could see them. They must be huge. He thought of church that Sunday morning and the message preached.

What is man that you should care for him?

He resolved to start going to church again. He had so much to learn. A Butter went inside and went to bed.

He slept well that night.

Chapter 18

Shawna and A Butter went to visit Jason as often as they could and they kept in touch by phone. Sometimes they used the phone in the Chinese man's shop for a small fee. Jason was a changed child full of hope and promise.

The teachers at the reform school spoke of his changed attitude to work and study and commended his parents. Rhona wrote him letters and Sean drew pictures for him which Jason used to decorate the space over his bed in the dormitory where he slept.

Shawna went to Curacao and bought costume jewelry and she also bought such jewelry from students at the school of art for sale downtown. At first sales were slow but picked up after a while as people from uptown came to the arcade to purchase cheaper goods.

A Butter was sometimes tired as study and work took its toll on him but he was determined to stay the course. He still taught on Sundays and some Saturdays, but spent a lot of time studying his own work and doing his assignments.

They were difficult for someone who had been out of the system for so long but he persisted.

In early November he got a telephone call. He was to attend the prize-giving ceremony of the Jamaica Cultural Development Commission and he was to read the poem *Escape into Love* at the ceremony.

Did that mean he had won a medal, he wondered? The person on the telephone said she couldn't let him know, he had to come to find out. The venue was a hotel in the New Kingston area and A Butter began to wonder what to wear. He wanted Shawna to be there too so he asked Mammy to take care of the children while they went to the award function.

A Butter put on his newest shirt and a pair of pants that Shawna had given him for his birthday, and Shawna dressed in a new dress she had bought in Curacao. They took a route taxi from Half Way Tree and walked the short distance to the hotel.

The room was all set up for the function and A Butter was asked to write his name in a register. He did this and both of them went inside and sat on the seats provided. Soon A Butter had to go on the platform where all those who had entered the competition were to sit. The room filled up fast.

After the welcome and introduction, the ceremony was in full swing. A Butter was nervous. He had to read his poem and it was such a long time since he had been asked to do that. He was breathing hard as he heard his name called and he learnt that his entry *Escape into Love* had won a gold medal. That settled the nerves. He was determined to read well.

And read well he did. He read his poem with feeling as though it came from his heart and the audience listened intently. The applause was tremendous. He sat down with his eyes glowing with happiness. A gold medal, he was on his way.

A Butter received his medal and was told to pick up a cheque at the commission's office. He had won ten thousand dollars, a windfall.

It was a proud George Butterfield who walked into the house at 22 Baker Street and showed his medal to Mammy and the children who would not go to sleep as long as their parents were away.

A Butter had difficulty sleeping that night as he was so happy he felt his heart pounding in his chest. He thought about the last eleven months and what it had brought him. It had brought him success but he knew it was just the beginning, not the end. He had a long way to go and he just hoped that he would continue on that pathway to bigger and better things. He slept only when Shawna held him close and said, "Sleep, you have work tomorrow."

It had been a good Wednesday night and Thursday lay before him, but before he slept he muttered to himself,

"Thank you, Father God."

Chapter 19

C hanges in A Butter and his family meant even more changes on Baker Street. It was said that people imitated that which was good and frowned sometimes on that which was less than wholesome. A Butter succeeded in his quest to become a teacher and joined the staff at the local primary school. But he did not forget the children on Baker Street and taught them all day on Saturdays. He became known as Teacher Butterfield and his fame spread as the man who could help almost all students to gain the highest grades in the Grade Six Achievement Test. A Butter went on to university and gained his degrees in education and was able to influence much of the island's education policy.

Determined to build on his gold medal-winning poem, A Butter worked on other poems and was able to see his first book published just after he completed his first degree.

Shawna was able to become an informal commercial importer. She was an astute businesswoman and had dreams of opening her own store later on in life. She remained relatively well in spite of the diabetes as she took her medication and stuck to her diet.

Jason completed his studies at HEART and he became a noted builder and contractor, building houses for people there in the inner city and elsewhere in the island. He never forgot his past and tried to build affordable houses for the people.

Rhona joined her father in the teaching profession and became the principal of a primary school in the countryside. She married and had children and, like her father, taught many children who succeeded in the Grade Six Achievement Test, moving on into high schools throughout her area.

Roly and Julie entered the HEART program and Roly had his own garage after studying in HEART and later at the automotive school. Julie became a chef and worked in hotels on the north coast.

Sean fulfilled his dream to become an artist and perhaps one could call him the most successful of them all. He went to the school of art where he excelled as a fine artist. Throughout the ensuing years he held art exhibitions and any of his pieces of work could be found all over the islands in the Caribbean.

Mammy's granddaughter became a nurse after going through high school and worked in the hospital downtown. Mammy died and was buried and received a loving tribute from the whole family, especially Rhona who remained forever grateful for the help that she had given.

But the success of the family stretched far and wide. Education became the main thrust for development on Baker Street. The community changed slowly but surely. Reluctant to leave the area that had made him and had nurtured his children, George Theophilous Butterfield bought the house that they had rented after Miss Kelly, the landlady, died and her children buried her. A Butter expanded and improved the house. The family planted flowers and vegetables as they removed the rusty gate and zinc fence and replaced it with a wall and a new gate.

Other house owners followed suit and the zinc fences were removed and replaced with concrete walls or hedges. The houses were repaired and beautified and the entire Baker Street began to look different from the ramshackle slum it had once been. The people of Baker Street were now proud of their street and were not afraid to say "I live on Baker Street".

All this occurred because one man stepped out of his dubious comfort zone and stretched out his hand to help himself up from the ground, and then help others to grow beyond their wildest dreams. If it could happen there, it could happen anywhere.

This was what changed the extraordinarily ordinary Baker Street.

Epilogue

Escape into Love

I see above me
The darkest night
And stars
That would impede my flight
I wish to soar
Above those clouds
Far away from angry moods
I long to walk
On midnights dark
And ease the moon
From its great height
To see me lonely and bereft
And longing for love
From the skies above
My eyes travel miles
Across the ocean's sky
And see an angel
That has seen my plight
It moves swiftly down
To touch the ground
Right there ahead
And I frown
But then I feel
A tiny touch
Not a hug
Or a hiss
But a gentle kiss
The angel speaks

And my knees are weak
As I fall to the ground
Forlorn and meek
Love first your God
And then yourself
Love too your neighbor
And your foe
Think not of hate
Nor to be great
Instead
Wear this crown of joy
Upon your head
Beyond the darkness
Are the stars
The pinpricks of light
Are greater by far
Than the fog that lies
Above earth's rim
That makes us see
Everything as dim
Your future lies
With the love you give
So give it all
And let fall
A goodness greater
Than all fame
All in God's name
I leave you now
My humble one
My duty I have now done
And with a whirl
And a flourish
The angel left
I stood and wept
At my past folly
And vowed then and there
To love unconditionally
Not just my neighbour

And my friend
But whoever else
Lies around the bend

George Theophilous Butterfield